RIDING WITH THE
LEADER OF THE PACK

A Read Easy-Ride Hard Story

By

T.J. Haynes

PUBLISHER'S NOTE

This book is fiction.

While the stories, locations and roads exist, the characters, dialog, descriptions and experiences are fiction and products of the author's imagination. Any resemblance to any real person, living or dead, or any real event or circumstance is strictly coincidental. Inclusion of the names of businesses, organizations or government offices in the story does not constitute endorsement by their officers or employees. Any reference to manufacturers or products does not constitute endorsement by or for the manufacturer or product.

RIDING WITH THE LEADER OF THE PACK

Published by
Posse Management Publishing
P.O. Box 781529, San Antonio, Texas 78278
www.possemanagement.com

ISBN-13: 978-0-9824700-0-8

Printed in the United States of America

Special pricing available for approved charities.
Send inquiries to info@possemanagement.com

Cover Photo by W. L. Haynes

ACKNOWLEDGEMENTS

Special thanks to editor Karl Monger of Austin, Texas. He is the best and a true professional!

Thanks also to Wanda Haynes, Norma Jean Lehr, Robert W. Spanogle, Bradley R. Wildey, Cheri Ray, William "Tunnel Rat" Haynes and Richard "Uncle Dick" Woods for their manuscript review, valued insight and recommendations.

To Wanda

Prologue

My name is Joshua Michael Dery, but you can call me Josh. A while back I was on a "lone wolf" ride through the South Texas Hill Country. It was a beautiful Sunday afternoon. Nature was flooding my senses with the brush of a warm wind, the smell of freshly harvested fields and a spectacular view of distant hills. Leaning and rolling down that twisting road headed nowhere in particular, I felt alert, alive and free.

Suddenly, around a corner came a pack of about twenty motorcycles. I extended my left arm out and low in the traditional, if not mysterious, greeting of the sport, but only two riders returned my salute. The others appeared unwilling to let go of very firm grips on both handlebars, and some were staring ahead so intently I wasn't sure they saw me at all.

As the rumble of their machines faded, my mind began racing. Who were they? Why did most of them seem so tense? What would possess someone to ride in a group if they weren't comfortable? How could someone accept the responsibility that comes with being the leader of such a pack? As my thoughts picked up speed, I realized my curiosity had taken over. There was little chance I could return to the solitude of my ride.

I found myself turning around and following them until they pulled into a dirt parking area next to what looked like an old barn. It turned out to be a makeshift roadside bar that catered to area weekend motorcyclists. Over the next forty-five minutes or so I mingled with the group. Although several wore vests or jackets with patches sewn on the back, indicating an affiliation with one riding organization or another, it was clear this was not a "club" ride.

In conversation I learned they had assembled that morning to participate in a charity run. Most of the riders did not know one another. One guy told me it was his first group ride, and his buddy nodded as though to say, "Same here." The person riding the front bike explained he had been asked by the charity to lead the group when he arrived that morning.

"They gave us a map, some people fell in behind me and off we went," he said.

Despite the fact that no one knew for sure who they were riding with, the group was enjoying itself at the stop and welcomed me unquestionably. They even asked me to join them for the remainder of the ride. I declined. They were a fun group, full of life and laughter. But, watching them depart, I concluded, based on facial expressions, motorcycle handling skills and general disorganization, that my decision not to ride with them was a sound one. They were clearly more comfortable socializing than riding. Two riders did stay behind, but in spite of obviously feeling intimidated, most were planning to "hang on tight" until they reached their next stop. The whole experience brought back memories.

The pack that interrupted my solitary ride that day was an example of the new generation of unlikely riding groups. They were together because they showed up at the same place and same time to support a charity. They had no knowledge of one another's riding skills or habits. Most had little or no group riding experience, and there were no leaders or rules or discipline. No one seemed to realize what they were doing would be unthinkable to the "bikers" they thought they were emulating.

So why would good and socially responsible people do something their elders in the sport wouldn't consider? I know the answer, because that's how I started riding. They had no idea they were doing anything wrong. They had passed a riding course, gained a little road experience and were participating for a good social reason, and a lot of other good people were with them. So what was the problem?

Like most of the riders in that group, I once thought freedom came as standard equipment with every motorcycle—more a birthright than a responsibility. I quickly learned to love the adrenalin rush that comes with speed and the feeling of power inherent in mastering a machine, but most of all I believed it was cool to be identified as a motorcycle rider. I wanted everyone to think I was just a little wild and carefree—at least on weekends.

I bought a motorcycle, dressed for success and hooked up with a group of riders whose main function was to reinforce one another's sense of belonging. Like most of my friends, I became part of the popular riding movement that I call the "ride to belong" crowd. In the process I made a decision to stay away from those who really do "live to ride or ride to live."

As a consequence, traditions, based on age-old lessons learned, were lost on me. I had no idea why traditional groups had so much structure or why rules, personal discipline and leadership responsibility were as serious to real bikers as riding skills. I would find out the hard way.

Born Leaders

I was born and raised in the small town of Junction, Texas. It's located on the northwest edge of the Texas Hill Country about 100 miles northwest of San Antonio, 450 miles southeast of El Paso and 150 miles northwest of Austin. Junction is a fairly typical west Texas town. With a population of around 2,600, our residents account for about half the people in Kimble County. Back in history, the area was pretty much a wild frontier territory with no real commercial attributes. There is, however, a natural junction where the north and south branches of the Llano River meet, and that's how the town got its name.

Until the 1850s there were few settlements in the area, which was generally regarded as just a good place to stop and rest if you were headed to San Antonio or felt the need to work up enough courage and energy to survive the long haul to El Paso. Not many people even took advantage of land grants during the time of the Republic of Texas, partly because the Apaches were still around. Eventually, however, a few adventurous souls moved in and some rich people from San Antonio started expanding their property holdings, and the area began to get settled.

While I was growing up ranching was still the biggest industry, but tourism and hunting have pretty much taken over these days. There are now twenty-three motels, eleven bed and breakfasts, exotic game ranches and a whole bunch of historic markers documenting our Wild West heritage. Even the Llano River State Park stays busy most of the year. But despite all the new activity and growth, it's still a frontier town down deep. We have only one traffic light, and other than London, Texas, which is much smaller than we are, there aren't any other settlements to speak of in the entire county.

Good thing, too, because it was a great place to grow up, especially if you have a passion for riding motorcycles, like me. There are hundreds of miles of winding roads in the Hill Country, endless trail riding in all directions and if you just want to get out and go fast, Interstate 10 has an eighty-mile-an-hour speed limit all the way to El Paso. There aren't many towns, trees or gas stations in that direction, though, so if you intend to make that run, I recommend planning your ride.

By 1995, I was twenty-four and had taken advantage of every riding opportunity our area had to offer. Because of the weather, we rode all year, and with over ten years experience I felt pretty confident as a rider. Like most small towns, we had two groups of motorcycle riders who got together on weekends. One group pretty much rode trails and occasionally organized races; the rest were road riders. I rode mostly with the trail riders until I went away to college. After I graduated, I came back home and noticed some interesting girls were joining the road group, so I bought a big sport bike.

We weren't a riding club or anything, just a bunch of people who started hanging out at the same place and riding together. The group was a mixture of ages and motorcycles. About two-thirds of the group rode some kind of bagger and the rest rode variations closer to my choice of equipment. In case you don't know, a bagger is slang for motorcycles with saddlebags. Motorcycle styles have changed over the years and some sport bikes now have bags, too, but those really don't count.

Sport bikes are popularly known as "crotch rockets" because the design makes you lean forward, thus you are riding on your crotch, rather than sitting on your ass. So if you're not sure which is which all you need to do is sit on the bike and let Mother Nature's pinch explain it to you.

Today, manufacturers classify motorcycles differently than riders actually talk so it can be confusing. For example, *cruisers* usually include Harleys, the Kawasaki Vulcan, Yamaha Roadstar, Honda Goldwing and the like. *Sport touring* normally means they kept the attributes of a sport bike but made it more comfortable for long rides, like the BMW R 1200 RT and such. *Sports bikes* include machines like the Honda CBR and Kawasaki Ninja series. They are built more for speed than distance. Riders I know don't bother to keep up with all the technical bullshit and just lump everything together as baggers, crotch rockets, choppers or dirt bikes. As I mentioned, I started riding on dirt bikes as a kid.

I switched to a crotch rocket when I joined the road group. You may have heard stories about groups that restrict participation to certain types of motorcycles, but we weren't that serious. We did have fun joking about one another's choice in rides, but we never really cared what you rode as long as it could keep up on the highway.

Back then, most of the riders in our group were

older than me, however, except for three or four guys no one had my riding experience. We were an unlikely assembly that defied demographic description. There was a computer programmer, a tow-truck driver, a secretary, a professor and a few students from the local Texas Tech campus along with a couple of guys who worked at the VA Hospital in Kerrville, just to name a few. Even our justice of the peace, who was known as "the orneriest cuss in Kimble County," rode a motorcycle and would occasionally stop by to check on us.

There were only two guys in our group who even came close to qualifying as real bikers. "Mad Dog" and "Fingers" both belonged to motorcycle clubs (or MCs, as they are known in the motorcycle world) at one time. Except for the story about how Fingers got his name, I didn't know much about them, which is typical with our group. Despite the fact that we were only weekend riders we all had riding names, which came about as the result of some twisted logic or circumstance. Fingers, for example, got his name while he was still riding with an MC over in Houston.

Fingers

As he explained it, in those days he always wore half-gloves. Half-gloves are the ones with the ends cut off so your fingers stick out. They are popular with many riders because they look tough and you don't need to take them off to get at stuff like you do with regular gloves. He was riding his chopper, wearing half-gloves, when his front tire blew and he lost control and fell off.

"Hell, I wasn't goin' that fast. I only skidded about ten feet," he says when he tells the story. "Didn't even hardly tear my jeans, but I put my hands down to cover my ass and the ends of these here three fingers got plum wore off."

He would continue, proudly displaying the three stubs on his left hand. "Been called 'Fingers' ever since," he would say, his tone more like that of someone accepting an award.

Mad Dog and Fingers would tell an occasional story about their days riding with MCs and were always trying to give the group advice. But we never took them seriously and considered their lectures more of a pain in the ass than a source of wisdom. After all, they were talking about the way their old groups did things, which included rules and procedures. Those weren't the kinds of things we thought fit the image of who we wanted to be. What we wanted to be was free.

My First Day as Leader of the Pack

Back then I viewed myself as one of the free-spirited people I had seen in Hollywood movies--at least on weekends. Like most people, I knew all *real* motorcycle groups had a "Leader of the Pack." So, when my "pack" asked me to be their "Road Captain," I thought it was pretty cool. For those who don't know, the Road Captain title has become a new-generation name of sorts for Hollywood's more infamous "Leader of the Pack."

The problem was my group didn't know why the position existed, only that we needed one if we were going to feel like—and be seen as—"bikers." Somehow the importance of the position was lost in the mystique of our movie image of riding. For us it was more like selecting a homecoming king. As for me, I felt like I had been voted most popular, which was important because I wanted desperately to impress one of the women who rode with us.

The day I was voted in as Road Captain, the group had decided to ride over to the Willow Creek Cafe, in Mason, for a late lunch. Mason is in the next county east of here. Since Junction was the only place in our county with real restaurants, making the forty-five-mile trip north on Highway 377 was a common ride for us.

We didn't know it at the time, but their sheriff had actually come to our county commissioners court to complain about our group. Evidently, he thought our county officials were sending us over there on weekends as part of a conspiracy against him. He claimed we were the reason his county had a higher accident rate than ours.

Even if we had known about his complaint, it wouldn't have mattered, because the moment we crossed the Kimble County Line, everyone breathed a little easier. The standard joke ran like this: If you are in a motorcycle accident, drag whatever you can across the county line. Simply laying there waiting for an ambulance would be a far more expensive and painful experience, because it meant a visit to our justice of the peace.

There really wasn't a conspiracy. We were just hungry and wanting to ride, so twelve of us jumped on our motorcycles and took off. I was disappointed that a girl named "Dakota," who I had my eye on, didn't ride with us, because I was leading for the first time. As it turned out, her decision not to go was for me a blessing in disguise.

En route, I was going a little fast and was forced

to hit my brakes hard to make a curve about a mile from the county line. In turn, the bike in back of me slammed on his brakes and swerved to avoid hitting my rear fender. Unfortunately, he swerved hard right and in the process hit the rear tire of the rider just behind me in the right lane position. By the time I looked in my mirror to see what all the commotion was about, six of the twelve motorcycles I had been leading were off the road and in the ditch. Despite the fact that I could see the county line up ahead, I decided the chance of a deputy showing up at that moment was slim. It didn't look like anyone was hurt, but I thought I should do the right thing, so I went back to the scene.

No one was hurt physically, but feelings were another matter. As soon as I got off my motorcycle, I saw two riders standing nose to nose arguing about the cause of the accident. The others were choosing sides and taking positions behind one rider or the other. I decided that, being the Road Captain, I should step in.

I thought I had everyone settled down when the rider who had almost collided with me got about eighteen inches from my face and said, "You asshole. This is your fault."

"My fault?" I responded. "Why don't you learn how to ride a motorcycle?"

He immediately hit me in the face and then wrestled me to the ground. We began rolling in the dirt punching and kicking each other until we heard the police siren. I would learn later that two of the other riders had called 911 as soon as the accident happened, without checking with anyone else. The dispatcher assumed it must be the real deal so they dispatched a sheriff's deputy, who was arriving fast. Needless to say he was none too happy with us, especially me.

The deputy was walking toward us when his cell phone rang. He talked into the phone and described the scene. After determining no one was hurt bad he went to his car and used the police radio to cancel the ambulance, which was already on the way.

When he got back to us he asked, "Does this mess have a leader?" Everyone pointed to me while I stood back, trying not to be obvious about my struggle to stop a nosebleed.

"You hurt?" he asked.

"No sir," I said.

He looked at all of us and shook his head. "Get your license and registration and come with me," he said.

"I wasn't in the accident," I said, thinking he was confused about who was involved.

"You the leader?" he asked.

"Yeah, I guess so," I said.

He shook his head again and said, "Get in the car." I got in.

While I was sitting in the car, I could see him outside talking on his cell phone. He walked back to the group and asked them some questions. Then he would talk on the cell phone again. After four or five minutes, he had the other riders check their bikes. Amazingly, they were all in working order, so he sent them on their way.

I watched through the windshield of the police car as they rode around the next corner headed for Mason and the Willow Creek Cafe, no doubt feeling relieved as they crossed the county line. I, on the other hand, was left wondering what the hell was going on.

The deputy was standing outside talking on his cell phone. He opened the door with the phone to his ear and said, "You have a couple of beers for breakfast?"

"No sir," I said.

"He says no, same as the rest," the officer said into his phone.

He listened for a while and then said, "Okay, got it," before joining me in the car.

"Young man," he said, "since no one was hurt and you managed to get your group in this mess while alcohol free, I'm going to let you go."

"Officer," I said, "I was not in the accident. What possible reason could you have for arresting me?"

"Were you going too fast when you approached the curve and slammed on your brakes or was the rider behind you speeding? How about failure to use your emergency flashers? Or the illegal U-turn you made to come back to the accident, or disorderly conduct?"

"What's going on?" I asked. "I didn't do anything."

"I said I was going to let you go," he repeated.

"Fine," I said. "Thank you! Give me my license back and I'm gone."

"Oh, by the way, Judge Houston wants to see you today," he added with a smile.

Judge Houston, our justice of the peace, was also known as "Hangman" among riders. He appeared to enjoy the riding name we assigned him, even though we never made it official. Normally, whenever we assigned someone a riding name we gave them a rocker, which is a patch with the name on it, for the back of their jacket or vest. In his case no one had the guts to do the presentation, so we just blew it off.

He didn't actually hang people, but we were all convinced that he would if the state legislature ever gave him the authority. "We got some strong trees down by the river," he was fond of saying. "Too bad those pissants in Austin won't let us use em' proper."

It was his idea of a joke, of course, but being ordered to see him was never a good thing.

"What?" I asked. "What the hell for?"

"I don't know," the officer said. "He must have heard the call on the radio. He called my cell and asked what was going on. I wanted to issue a couple citations, but he said to let everyone go and have you stop by and see him. This must be your lucky day," he said with a sarcastic smile. He was well aware that my day was not going to get any better.

"By the way," he said, "if you try to lead another group anywhere before he releases you, he told me I should take you directly to jail."

"This is bullshit," I said. "Just give me my license." I hesitated before adding, "Please."

He handed me my license and maintained a knowing smile. He was clearly enjoying this moment… unlike me.

I went back to my motorcycle and decided I should go to Mason and check on the group before I went to see Hangman. When I arrived at the Willow Creek Cafe, everyone had already ordered lunch and was waiting to be served. They were still talking about the accident, but all had been forgiven and the conversation had turned jovial—a few jokes, teasing one another for having screwed up and eventually turning the whole thing into a bonding experience that would become part of the group's folklore.

It wasn't the first time there was trouble on a ride, and everyone figured it was just part of riding. As usually happens, the guy who punched me apologized, I accepted, we hugged and it was over. I was surprised, however, when he said, "Man, thanks for handling that cop! I thought for sure he was going to give me a ticket.

Must be nice to be a reporter and have some pull." I had been working as a reporter for our local newspaper only since graduating from college two years before. I had no "pull" anywhere. But if the group wanted to think I had "handled the cop" that was fine by me.

I had already decided I would make an excuse to ride back alone. I wanted to avoid explaining why I couldn't lead them on the return trip. I also had no intention of having a beer, just in case the deputy was hanging around the county line waiting for me.

"No problem," I said. "We just called Hangman and he took care of everything. I need to run over to his place and thank him so I'm headed out."

"Go for it, Captain," he said. I left feeling like a genius. It was a feeling that wouldn't last long.

Hangman's Sentence

Every county in Texas has between one and eight justices of the peace, depending on the population, and they mostly handle class C misdemeanors and minor civil stuff. But sometimes they run things differently in small counties like ours that only have one JP. Hangman used his distinction as the only JP to be in charge of whatever suited his mood, a fact that usually ended up scaring the hell out of citizens and pissing off the county commissioners. He wore his image of "ornery" the same way Texas Rangers wear their badges. With pride! The only reason he kept getting reelected was because no one had the balls to run against him.

Hangman didn't have a real office. He mostly sat on his front porch and waited for "customers" to be delivered by the sheriff's department. Everyone knew, if he was on the porch sitting in his chair with a shotgun within reach, he was open for business. If he wasn't, you were expected to wait until he was. When I rode up he came out of the house, shotgun in hand, and starting talking before I was fully dismounted.

"What the hell you think you're doin'?" he asked.

He was a huge man with a big gut—the kind that only comes from a complete avoidance of physical labor and drinking enormous amounts of beer. Despite the sloppy physique his hair was kept neatly short under his ever-present brown cowboy hat. He had a trimmed but full beard that was specked with gray, and he wore his usual long-sleeve Western shirt, blue jeans and pointed toe boots. He had been the JP since I was about ten years old so I guessed he was probably in his mid fifties, but it was hard to tell because a perpetual scowl kept at bay any detailed observation of his face.

"The deputy said you wanted to see me?" I asked as I removed my helmet.

"You think I'm stupid? I know why you're here. I want to know why you were leadin' the group today."

"They elected me Road Captain," I said.

"That election must a' been asshole deep in Democrats," he said.

"Sir," I said, trying to be respectful, "I don't understand your point.

"Ain't no equal opportunity around here. You either know your shit or you don't. And you don't. Only a bunch of liberals would be dumb enough to allow you to lead a motorcycle ride," he said. Needless to say, there weren't many Democrats left in our county in those days, and Abraham Houston (his real name) was well known for freely sharing his decidedly strange independent views. When Bill Clinton was first elected, they say he wrote the mayors of both towns named Clinton, Texas—one in Dewitt County and one in Hunt County—recommending they change their names "for the good of Texas." He was quick to justify his every idea by claiming to have inherited his wisdom from Sam Houston, one of Texas' founding fathers, who he claimed as a relative.

"Hey," I said, feeling myself growing irritated, "I've been riding--"

"Long enough to lead that group into a ditch. Cut the crap. Court is in session." He rapped his knuckles against the table next to his chair to make it formal then added, "You don't have enough experience to piss from the Pecos Bridge without gettin' your boots wet."

"Your honor," I said, "I don't know why I'm here. Am I being charged with something?"

"Son," he said, "I reserve the chargin' for those damn Northerners. They got the pissants in Austin all turned around lookin' at Mexico while they sneak across our borders from the east and buy up the whole damn state. Some of 'em's even movin' in around here. Hell, I don't have time to watch those low crawlin' snakes and you, too. I ain't chargin' you. I'm telling you. We ain't got enough native Texans left around here to let you kill off everybody on a motorcycle. You ain't qualified to lead a turd to an outhouse hole, and until Big Lou tells me you know what you're doin', you ain't leadin' nobody nowhere. You understand, or do I need to warm up a brandin' iron and write it on your ass?"

Everyone in the county knew who Big Lou was.

"Big Lou?" I said, involuntarily. "I've ridden with him a few times. What's he got to do with me?"

"Young man, you tell me another lie an' the county's gonna own that motorcycle over there."

"Yes sir," I responded, my eyes glued to my boots.

The truth was I'd never really ridden with Big Lou, but I had swapped a few stories with other riders in my group. If you were a rider in our town it was more important to know Big Lou than the details of the motorcycle you were riding. Trying to save a little face I said, "I know a lot about him. But what's he got to do with me?"

"Rumors," he said, shaking his head. "You don't know a damn thing about Big Lou except rumors. You know the difference between rumors and farts, Mr. Smart Ass Reporter?"

"No sir, I don't," I replied, assuming I was about to get one of his famous philosophical summations on life.

"Not a damn thing," he replied. "They both float around silently doing their damage 'til someone yells FART and opens a window." He laughed as if completely amused with himself, then quickly became serious again. "Go see Big Lou. He'll open a few windows for ya. You might even learn to like the fresh air. Don't come back here 'til he says you know what you're doin'."

I was completely confused and pissed off by this whole situation. I had no interest in going to see Big Lou. He was the one person more feared than Hangman in our county. I reminded myself that despite his fondest wishes, this was no longer the Wild West. There was nothing legal about any of this. But I had been raised here, and I knew resisting would put me on a level with the ACLU, which most people around here regarded with as much affection as they did cancer. Some argued it was cancer. I knew he had me by the balls and so did he.

"Yes sir," I said. "I'll go see him right now. I've got a ride to lead next Sunday," I added.

"You ain't leadin' shit 'til Big Lou tells me it's okay." With that he banged his knuckles on the table again and said, "Court's adjourned. Git!"

"Yes sir," I said, and walked back to my motorcycle. Despite the courtesy I showed him, I had no respect for the fat old bastard. I knew how to ride, and I didn't appreciate him inferring otherwise. It was insulting and potentially embarrassing if the group found out. But along with being pissed, I was also afraid of what he might do if I simply ignored his order. I decided I had no choice but to go see Big Lou.

Big Lou and the Sheriff

You could call "Big Lou" a living legend among motorcycle riders in my county. His name was dropped into riding stories as casually and often as a chef sprinkles salt while cooking. Despite the fact that he was never around when the tales were told, I never once heard anyone ask who he was. Professing to know him was a badge of experience, and to motorcyclists around here it was experience that determined your place in our social order, at least on weekends. I myself had been known to include his name in an occasional riding story. Since no one I knew had actually been seen with him—except for Hangman and the sheriff—I saw little danger in dropping his name.

Legend had it, when he first rode into town he looked pretty bad. It was assumed back then that anyone with his scruffy road-worn appearance, dressed in leather and on a motorcycle, was scouting for a pack of "outlaw bikers," who were bound to arrive soon. When you live in a small town like ours, people worry about such things. Maybe it's because all the places that got overrun by bad guys in the movies reminded us of our hometown, or because our security has always been most threatened by outsiders. First it was bands of Apache, then the Mexicans, then Austin government and rich guys from San Antonio, then speculators from the east and the United States government. They had all inflicted their damage so we were never really secure enough to let our guard down, even for motorcycle riders.

To complicate matters, kids were attracted to Big Lou's tough guy image and his motorcycle. This was before video games hit their full stride around here so children still actually played outside and would gather wherever he parked. At first, parents believed the pied piper of evil had arrived, and everyone was concerned. But instead of creating unrest, he settled into a quiet life on the edge of town near the race track. He would ride off, sometimes for a month or two, but he always returned. To make things more confusing, he and our sheriff developed a strange friendship.

Sheriff Gonzalez

Sheriff P.J. Gonzalez was an imposing figure of a man. He was about six feet five inches tall, and unlike most Texas sheriffs he didn't appear to have an ounce of fat on him. He was about the same age as Hangman, but his close-cut hair was dark brown with just a speck of gray showing under his ever-present white Stetson. Besides being in shape, the other thing that set him apart from other elected lawmen was he never carried a gun. For this he had a simple explanation: "Don't figure I need one for this job. I just make sure everyone else is pointin' theirs in the right direction." The words were always accompanied by a trademark smile that exuded a strength that only comes from unquestionable personal confidence.

He had retired from the Texas Rangers when I was about eight and was elected sheriff shortly thereafter. He had been in office ever since and had been challenged only twice, both times by former deputies he had fired at different times for what he called "pissin' on citizens." He won in a landslide each time, so I guess most people agreed with him. The other thing that made him popular was the clever ways he handled problems in the county.

We have a very small county jail, and one year the state inspector came in and complained that it was overcrowded. At the same time a preacher in town had lost his flock. We have a lot of churches around here, so competition is stiff, and this guy was known to be very long-winded. Word was, if you went to his church on Sunday morning you needed to pack a lunch. The poor guy would drone on for hours and sometimes even get "moved by the spirit" and wind up talking in tongues. The sheriff, who prided himself on knowing everyone and everything that happened in the county, saw an opportunity.

He hired the preacher as the jail chaplain and made the inmates attend his services every morning. His sermons, which were presented in the jail cafeteria, rolled right on through lunchtime. Hangman even complained publicly that his revenue was dropping because that preacher "brought hell right to the jailhouse." There were a few complaints from out-of-town "guests," but generally speaking nobody cared. People around here thought it was a good idea. Especially Fingers, because that's where he found Jesus.

As the story goes, a few weeks after Big Lou arrived, a pack of motorcycles showed up at the London Dance Hall out on Highway 377. The hall was located in London, Texas, a small town about nineteen miles north of Junction, and only opened on Friday and Saturday nights. It had a saloon, pool tables and a big dance hall with a live band that played everything from the Beer Barrel Polka to the Cotton-Eyed Joe. It was the best place around for real Texas Swing and cold beer, although you sometimes had to be patient if you wanted something particular. The pack of riders who showed up weren't used to waiting and created such a commotion that the bartender called the police. Sheriff Gonzalez responded but was heavily outnumbered, so he hesitated to go inside. Instead he called for backup and waited outside.

As the sheriff tells it, while he was waiting for backup outside London Hall, Big Lou rode up, dismounted, looked at him and said, "Need backup?"

The sheriff said, "They're on the way."

Big Lou said, "Good," and walked straight into the bar. A few minutes later out came Big Lou with one of the riders. "Sheriff, this here's Dingo. He's the leader of this bunch. He and I go way back."

The sheriff said, "Nice to meet you," and put out his hand, but Dingo didn't take it.

Then Big Lou quickly said, "Dingo, this here's a friend of mine. He and I and some of our friends will be goin' in for a beer in about five minutes if you care to join us."

Dingo said, "No disrespect, sheriff—any friend of Big Lou's is good with me—but I need to get my boys saddled up."A few minutes later they left and never came back.

The sheriff and Big Lou went in for a beer and ended up staying so long they called a deputy to drive them both home. Some of the people in London Hall that night claim Dingo actually pulled a gun when Big Lou walked in. But Big Lou just ignored it and walked right up to him and said something. No one could hear what he said, but Dingo put his gun away, told his gang to settle down and the two of them walked outside. When their leader went back in and told the group to saddle up, one of the guys said, "We need to waste that son of a bitch." Dingo smashed a beer bottle, held it up to the guy's face and said, "I said saddle up. You didn't see him, and we ain't ever comin' back here."

The sheriff never told anyone what he and Big Lou talked about, but they were seen together once in a while, sitting in the back corner of various places in town eating or drinking a beer. Every so often Hangman would be with them, too.

More About Big Lou

Alternately Big Lou was rumored to be the former leader of a notorious motorcycle gang or a crazy war veteran. The truth is no one knew who he was, where he came from or why he chose our town to settle down. Nobody ever saw him without his motorcycle, and everywhere he stopped, kids would gather. He would occasionally surprise one inspecting his motorcycle. They were usually so intrigued by his machine they failed to notice he was approaching or that the other kids were running for their lives. He would always grab the unfortunate one by the shirt and begin his interrogation.

"Hey boy," he would say, "where is the carburetor on my machine?" Or, "What kind of brakes are these? How can you ride a motorcycle if you don't know how they work?"

Startled by being jerked from their riding fantasy, some ran away in tears. Others just stood there wide-eyed until they came to their senses and ran off vowing to learn the answers. In time parents began insisting their children answer his questions before they would let them ride. I remembered my own frightening experience, so I knew that part of the legend was true.

Also, one of my first assignments as a reporter was covering the theft of two motorcycles. The story became a real life mystery. It was unusual for motorcycles—or much of anything else—to be stolen around here. And since I am a reporter and a motorcycle rider I was assigned to cover the story.

The police report stated that the theft occurred in the early morning hours behind the Legend Inn, a popular overnight stop for out-of-town riders. But the owners of the bikes were listed in the report as unknown. Rumor had it one of the motorcycles belonged to our justice of the peace. But no one would verify who owned either motorcycle or why they were parked at the Legend overnight. Here's the real strange part. That afternoon, people saw Big Lou and the sheriff sitting in the back corner at the Junction Restaurant. Later that day two people reported seeing Big Lou ride out of town.

He came back six days later, and as close as I can tell, about an hour after he arrived, two guys in a pickup and trailer with two motorcycles pulled into the sheriff's office parking lot, unhooked the trailer and took off. The one deputy who happened to get a look at the guys said, "They looked like they had been in a bad accident or had the shit beaten out of 'em." Anyway, the motorcycles were reported returned to whoever owned them. Not only were all the parts intact, they had been cleaned. The trailer, which had a New Mexico plate, was sold in the next sheriff's auction.

I interviewed the sheriff and everyone else involved, except Big Lou, and no one professed to know anything other than what I am telling you. Hangman denied it was his motorcycle that was stolen outside the Legend

Inn. I always believed Big Lou had something to do with recovering those bikes, but never quite got up the guts to go ask. Now that I had no choice but to visit him, I made a note to include that in my questions.

First Meeting

I had finished college, served an internship as a reporter and was now a gainfully employed adult. I thought I was doing all right for my age. I was accustomed to getting what I wanted and felt confident. Yet the thought of confronting Big Lou was more than a little unsettling. It wasn't something I would even consider if I had a choice. But, thanks to my big mouth, I had given my friends the impression that I knew him intimately. Plus, the JP made it clear getting his approval was the only way I could continue as the leader of our group. How could I tell anyone I didn't want to talk to a legend I already professed to know? I couldn't. So when I found myself walking down that gravel driveway leading to the front door of his house, my heart was pounding.

The house was not more than twenty feet from a detached metal shed and less than one hundred yards from the back of our community's dirt race track. I had passed by his place a thousand times, but the thought of stopping had never occurred to me. In fact, the only time I did actually talk to him was when my mother had taken me to meet him in the shed next to his house, when I was fourteen.

My mother was a single parent and worked a lot, so I was without supervision most of the time, especially in the summer. Probably out of guilt, she had scraped together enough money to meet my demand for a dirt bike. The only catch was that I had to go with her to talk about riding with Big Lou. In the last few minutes I had scoured my memory for details of that encounter, but nothing came to mind, except for a sense of being very afraid.

As I approached the front door and raised my hand to knock, I heard a voice.

"Over here."

It was coming from the shed, so I turned and headed in that direction. The shed looked old and worn, but I noticed the fixtures and rails of the two sliding doors were well maintained. The doors were open, and as I approached I could make out the shadowy figure of a man inside. The sun was shining brightly, and it was darker inside than outside, so it took a few seconds for my eyes to adjust.

"Would ya see better without those sunglasses, punk?" the voice said.

Shit, I'm an idiot, I thought, taking off my sunglasses.

Standing before me was Big Lou. He looked old or maybe just hard. His face was like carved leather. It was a look only decades of overexposure to the sun and wind can create. He had a full head of long hair pulled back into a ponytail and matching full beard. Both were white. I judged he was at least six feet four. Despite his age and substantial shoulders and arms, his stomach wasn't overly large, giving him the appearance of someone fit and strong. He was dressed in well worn jeans and a shirt with a motorcycle decal. For some reason I was surprised by the fact that his shirt had a collar. I found myself wondering if I had a motorcycle shirt with a collar. I couldn't think of any.

"Yo, man. 'Sup?" I said, trying desperately to sound

casual.

"Ya always disrespectful, punk?" he asked.

Evidently the crusty old guy was offended by my greeting, but I couldn't think of anything else to say. I noticed his hands looked huge but weren't as dirty as I had expected. I thought to myself, *There is nothing here to be afraid of, so why is my heart still pounding*? He was obviously growing impatient with my lack of response, not to mention the deer in the headlights expression on my face, so he pressed on.

"What do ya want?" he asked coldly.

The Hangman told me to come see you," I blurted out.

"Think he's pissed at you or me?" he asked.

"Me," I said. "He doesn't think I know how to lead a motorcycle ride."

"Do ya think yer a leader, punk?" he asked.

I felt a nervous hesitation as I said, "Hey, I didn't cause the accident."

He ignored my response. "Do ya think yer a leader? Yes or no?" he said with a firmness that communicated, *Cut the bullshit.*

"Yes," I found myself saying quickly.

"Why?" he followed up.

I had asked myself this question while trying to anticipate our conversation. "Well, I think I can ride well enough, and the group asked me if I would be the Road Captain."

"Mmmm," he responded as he moved toward me looking me straight in the eye. His eyes were clear and brown with a piercing quality that made it feel as though he were looking straight into my brain. I suddenly remembered how those eyes had challenged my entire being as a child. I remembered looking down in an attempt to escape their power. I decided I would not look away this time so I forced myself to meet his challenge.

"Riding is riding and a group is a group, ya know what I mean, punk?" he said.

I was startled again. *What kind of question is that*? I thought to myself. Rather than risk irritating him with a slow response, I resorted to honesty. "I'm not exactly sure what you mean," I blurted out as my eyes involuntarily looked down.

As soon as I looked down he said, "Come back when ya know," then he turned and walked away shaking his head.

It was obvious our interview was over. I decided to give it one last try. "Hey," I said, "is that a trick question?"

No response.

"Where can I find the answer?"

No response.

In desperation I asked, "When can I come back?"

"When ya know the answer," came the response, followed by the sound of metal banging against metal. He had gone back to whatever work he was doing when I arrived.

As I walked back to the paved lot next to his property, I started to get pissed. At first, I was upset with myself, but slowly I began to transfer my anger to Big Lou and what I concluded was a stupid question on his part. *Riding is riding and a group is a group*. What the hell did that mean?

3

The Nature of Riding and Groups

When I left Big Lou's place I decided to ride a while to clear my mind. Actually, it was more like hiding. The group would be back at our usual hangout by now, but I was in no mood to face what was sure to be a bunch of unsympathetic smartasses. I loved being with them and we usually had a great time together, but they could be brutal, especially when you did something really stupid. They would want to know about my "thank you" visit to Hangman, and I couldn't tell them he had forced me to meet with Big Lou or what happened at the meeting. I had convinced myself that none of this was my fault. But I could still feel the trap, commonly buried in little white lies, closing in on me.

Riding with my bruised ego that afternoon just added to my confusion. At one point, I had to make a radical swerve to avoid some idiot on a cell phone who had failed to properly negotiate a curve and was coming at me head on. I reacted instinctively, swerving onto the shoulder, around an old tire tread and back onto the road without hesitation. I knew how to ride. *What the hell was Big Lou's problem*? I thought to myself. This whole thing was bullshit, and I intended to get out of it. But how?

Technically, I had visited him as the Hangman ordered. But I couldn't answer his question, and he told me to come back. *Maybe I should just blow the old bastard off*? I thought. I hardly ever saw any of my group during the week, so I decided to forget about it for a few days. I was sure I'd figure out something eventually.

Trouble at Work

I went to work on Monday as usual, but the problem with Big Lou was consuming me. I couldn't figure out what to do, and the answer to his question totally eluded me. I felt trapped. I had a tendency, back then, to over-think things when I had a problem. I would mentally turn a minor trouble into a full-blown crisis, only to discover later that it didn't matter to anyone else either way. This was especially true if I stood to be proven wrong. If I felt threatened I focused the full force of my curious nature and penchant for research on proving I was right. The alternative—failure—was just too humiliating.

Fortunately, my job did not involve the critical care of other people, so lack of attention to my work wouldn't do any immediately noticeable harm. The *Junction Journal* was published weekly, and it was by any standard no big deal. But as a new graduate with a journalism degree it was a place to start. In addition to reporting on local business and crime, I was in charge of setting up our first web site. The paper was actually printed in San Angelo, but our local staff of eight did all the other work. Like most newsweeklies we were struggling to survive, and when that happens little problems are sometimes blown out of proportion. I fit right in.

Early Wednesday morning, I was called into a meeting with the publisher, the sales director and my boss, who was also my editor. I had been around long enough to suspect this was not going to be good news. I was right. They informed me that one of my recent articles had created quite a stir with the CEO of one of our biggest advertisers and wondered what I planned to do about it. I told them I didn't intend to do anything. After a little discussion, the publisher said, "Look, you are a good reporter. Don't take this personally, it's just business. Business is business and reporting is reporting. They are different things. We are in the business of reporting so until you understand the business you will only be half as good as you could be."

Immediately I came out of my chair. At long last it came to me. I understood Big Lou's question. I thanked them, told them I would take care of it and left. They thought I was going to write a retraction or call the advertiser, but I had something else in mind—something more important to me.

I had taken a course on group dynamics in college, and I was going to do a little research. I would worry about the other problem later. I spent the rest of the morning on my computer, making and transcribing notes and my thoughts. I finally realized Big Lou's question was not that complicated. Riding required the coordination of physical and mental skills. I knew that. Participation in groups isn't physical at all; it requires social and communication skills. I had never thought about it like that. So I wrote:

> *Riding in a group is more complicated than riding alone, because a whole new set of variables are introduced. They are social in nature, not physical. No wonder our rides are always so screwed up.*

I remembered something Fingers always said when comparing his old MC to our group. "We're nothing but a bunch of lone wolves. Ain't nothin' more dangerous to a pack than a lone wolf. My old club wouldn't allow it." I decided to run over to his place and pick his brain before going to see Big Lou.

Fingers' Wisdom

Fingers operated a wrecker service out of the garage next to his house trailer. He had one old tow-truck he brought with him when he arrived in town. He moved to Junction from Houston about a year before I returned home from college. He and his wife had three kids and not a lot of business. He was about forty years old and, except for the fact that he was very skinny, looked every bit the part of a biker. He had long flowing hair and a thin Fu Manchu mustache. His face was otherwise clean shaven but pitted, and he always wore a skull cap and round silver earrings. He had tattoos up and down both arms, but other than a skull-and-crossbones on his right forearm, all the art was faded and no longer distinguishable. His wife was a very sweet person and about four or five times the size of Fingers. Most of us agreed she was about as large as her hometown of Comfort, Texas, which is located between Junction and San Antonio. The group gave her the riding name "Comfort" about a month after they started riding with us and she loved it, though I don't think she knew the story behind it.

It was quite a sight to see the two of them on his old chopper. There was no passenger seat, so Comfort just sat on the fender. When she did this the entire fender would disappear under her bulk. But it must have been reinforced somehow because it never bent and always reappeared, unmarred, whenever she got off.

I never once heard her complain, although if a vehicle happened to be traveling with us she was usually in it. The two of them always appeared to enjoy riding with the group or just hanging around rallies, but they seldom joined us at Isaack's Restaurant, our regular weekend gathering place.

Fingers also freelanced as a motorcycle mechanic, doing basic maintenance for cash, so I decided to have him change my oil as an excuse for stopping by. He was home when I got there and immediately began working on my bike.

"What was it like to be in an MC?" I asked.

"Safe," he said.

"I thought you didn't like rules."

"Don't like politics and government rules. They are the devil's wrenches."

"I thought MCs had a lot of rules," I said.

"Mostly they just follow God's law."

"What do you mean?"

"You guys don't understand," he said. "Ya put a lone wolf in a pack a riders and there'll be trouble. No way to avoid it. It's one of God's laws. MCs know that, so they have rules to keep everybody safe. When ya join they put ya on probation, make ya prove yer loyal to the group, teach ya the rules and train ya to ride their way. They wouldn't even think about ridin' with a bunch like y'all. That's why I always hang back anywhere we go."

"Why?" I asked. "Don't you think we can ride?"

"Don't get me wrong," he said immediately. "Ain't nothin' wrong with bein' a lone wolf rider. It ain't personal. Got nothin' to do with ridin' neither," he said, "just survivin'. God's law warns us it ain't safe to ride in a group when everybody has their heads up their own asses. MCs just make sure ya put the group first. Ya know what I mean? Do unto others, that's all."

It took a little time to understand Fingers and the way he looked at life, but he had at least confirmed what I was looking for. MCs were structured to manage both riding skills and social challenges.

"Why'd you leave the club?" I asked.

"Comfort got homesick. Didn't matter to me or my truck where we worked, so we moved back here. Since we found Jesus, we talked about joinin' the Christian Bikers in Kerrville, but she don't wanna ride bitch that far without a seat. I told her she already has the best seat in Kimble County," he said, and began to snort with uncontrollable laughter. I looked around to make sure Comfort wasn't nearby and joined in.

I had gotten the information I was after, so when he finished changing my oil I excused myself.

"I have to head over to see Big Lou," I said.

"That's cool," he responded. "He and I used to ride together a lot. Tell 'im I said 'hey'."

I knew he was telling a little white lie and meant no harm. He thought I was telling one, too, and he was just joining in the fun. I took off for Big Lou's.

Answering the Question

It was 5:30 in the afternoon when I pulled into the parking lot next to Big Lou's place. It was still light outside, but a light was on in his house. Unlike the day before, I was excited as I walked down that gravel road and knocked on his door. The excitement faded fast when he opened the door, stared me straight in the eye, and said, "Why are ya here, punk?"

Without thinking, I said, "I think I know the answer to your question." I kept my gaze strong and confident.

"If ya just *think* ya know, why are ya here?" Then he shut the door.

As I stood there for a couple of seconds in a state of semi-shock, I played back what I had just said.

"Shit! I don't *think.* I'm sure I know." The words blasted out of my mouth so fast and loud, I wasn't aware if I said them or thought them. Big Lou opened the door and said, "Come in."

His living room was a lot neater than I had imagined. Except for the fact there was a motorcycle parked where a television would take up space in most homes and nothing on the walls, it looked pretty normal. There was a couch, a chair, a coffee table, a lamp, and a hardwood floor that looked clean enough to eat off of. He was dressed in newer jeans than the day before and a different collared motorcycle shirt. I reminded myself once again to check to see if I had a riding shirt with a collar.

As I stood there awkwardly looking around, he closed the door and came around to stand in front of me. Again looking me square in the eye, he said, "So tell me."

Determined to meet his challenge, I returned his gaze and said, "Riding a motorcycle and leading a group are two different things. Riding requires an understanding of the laws of gravity and is physical and mental. Leading a group is not physical at all. It requires social skills and an understanding of the nature of groups and basic human communications." Suddenly my mind was spinning and my mouth was blurting information before I had a chance to consider it clearly. "None of the dynamics of a group environment go away because we are on motorcycles. In fact, they are accelerated—"

"You clean the bullshit out before ya put on yer brain bucket?" he interrupted, pointing to my head, "or do ya ride like that?"

"What do you mean?" I asked.

He ignored my question and motioned to the couch. "Have a seat. Ya want somethin' ta drink?"

"Sure," I said, and he left the room. While he was gone, I thought about what I had said and what I had discovered in my research. I knew I was right. I had been on so many rides like the one that landed me here. Some were embarrassing, some were downright dangerous, and most were no fun at all. I got his point but didn't understand what his problem was.

When Big Lou returned, he sat in a chair that conformed perfectly to his body—like a tailor-made suit—and he looked completely at ease.

"Do you have any questions for me, punk?" he asked, once again catching me completely off guard. I thought for a few seconds and, unlike the day before, he waited, showing no signs of being impatient. Then it came to me. This was my opportunity.

"So, how did you recover Hangman's motorcycle?" I asked in my best reporter's voice.

"Ya askin' as a motorcycle rider or a punk-ass reporter?" he asked.

I thought about the question for a second and decided there was no reason to report whatever he had to say. "I'm just a curious motorcycle rider."

"Mmmm. A curious motorcycle rider," he said. "Ya think ya can blame yer motorcycle for stickin' yer nose in other people's business, punk?"

He was starting to piss me off again, so I decided to change the subject.

"Okay then. What was wrong with my answer earlier?" I asked.

"Did you like your answer?" he asked, speaking

very formally.

"Yeah," I said. "I get it."

"Do I talk like that?" he asked.

"Like what?" I asked. "I was answering your question." He was really irritating me.

"If it was my question, why didn't ya answer it the way I talk? Ya expect me to learn how to talk like you to get the answer to my own question?" he asked.

"Look," I said, feeling frustrated. "Can we change the subject? I really don't know what this has to do with my leading a motorcycle ride. What is the most important thing to know about leading a group?" I asked.

"What do you think?" he replied.

"I think it's understanding people and how they function in groups," I said.

"How do ya do that?" he asked.

"I guess by studying. I took a course on group dynamics in college," I responded, knowing before I said it he would not like my answer. But it was the only one I had.

He shook his head in disgust and stared at me.

"You've been studying yer whole life, ya have a college education, so why is it ya don't know shit about people?"

"Why you raggin' on me?" I was pissed off and sounded it, but I couldn't keep looking into his eyes. They were just too powerful. So I dropped my head to break off contact.

As soon as my eyes hit the floor he got up from his chair, picked up my glass and headed to what I assumed was the kitchen. "Why ya wastin' my time, punk?" he said in a mocking tone.

Unwilling to give up, I said, "Look, how long does

this take? I mean, I just came here because I was ordered to. How many more questions do I need to answer?"

"You always follow people around uninvited?" he asked. His voice was calm and his tone was neutral, but he had turned and was looking me straight in the eye again, challenging me. But he didn't call me a punk this time. I suddenly realized I had followed him into the kitchen.

"I'm sorry," I said, looking down to escape his challenge. "I'm just worried I won't be able to lead the group this weekend."

"Why does that worry you?" he countered.

"Hey, man, it's embarrassing. Know what I mean? I've been riding since—"

"Since ya were fourteen," he interrupted. "I know." He held my intimidated gaze with his self-assured one. "You were a pretty self-centered and insecure little asshole, as I remember, but I figured ya would outgrow it. Have ya?"

"What the hell does that mean?" I said, feeling my blood start to boil.

"Have ya, punk?" he asked again. I could feel him looking at me, but I couldn't look up. When I didn't respond he said, "Guess not."

His words felt like they were cutting into my very soul. I could feel an urge to smash his leathery face with my fist as anger welled up from deep inside me. It wasn't a rage I felt often, but when it comes it quickly becomes uncontrollable.

"Go to hell, you asshole!" I said, turning to get out of there as quickly as I could. I stormed out the front door, slamming it hard against the frame, and walked like a madman back to my motorcycle. My hands were shaking so hard I could barely get the key in to start it. Still filled with rage, I pulled out of the parking lot and hit the throttle hard. I heard my rear tire scream and felt the front end lift up. That's the last thing I remember.

When I woke up I was in an ambulance that was just beginning to move. I sat up to look out the window. My head throbbed painfully, and I saw my motorcycle and a car on the side of the road, some flashing lights, and in the distance was Big Lou, standing there shaking his head. *I'll get that son of a bitch,* I thought to myself. *He caused this.*

They kept me overnight in the hospital, but other than a slight concussion and some pretty bad road rash on my left side I was okay. No bones were broken. From what I could see from the ambulance, my motorcycle had survived, too. Evidently, when I left the parking lot, a car was pulling out of a driveway just down the road. The driver didn't know I had hit the throttle hard. She misjudged my speed and pulled out onto the street. My front wheel was in the air slightly and obstructed my view, and by the time it came down and I saw the slow-moving car ahead of me it was too late. To avoid hitting it I swerved, but I must have hit my brakes or some loose gravel. Anyway I went down hard. The police estimated I slid for about 20 feet. The hospital staff presented me with my leather jacket, gloves, and helmet, all of which were destroyed when I hit the pavement and slid. Unfortunately, it was a work day and I hadn't bothered to change so I still had dress slacks on. It would take a while for the skin on my hip and leg to heal.

Putting First Things First

I took the next couple of days off, more out of self-pity than medical necessity, and called some of my friends to let them know I wouldn't be riding over the weekend. They already knew about the accident. Word—fact or fiction—travels fast in our town. On Sunday the group rerouted their ride to include a stop by my place to wish me well. All in all it was damned embarrassing. I still hurt some, but mostly I was just feeling sorry for myself. The only good news was that no one knew about my trouble with Big Lou and I had a lot of time to think about everything.

I knew what happened was my own fault but was having a hard time admitting it. Between pain pills, I tried to blame the car for failing to judge my speed correctly. But the reporter in me asked how the driver could have known my emotions were twisting the throttle and I would be speeding ahead at an unreasonable pace. Then there was Big Lou. I tried to hate the bastard, but what had he really done? He asked a couple of questions about leading a group that, for reasons that still eluded me, he thought were important. He wanted to know why I had gone into his kitchen uninvited and if I had changed from the self-centered fourteen-year-old he once met.

I, on the other hand, was looking for a quick way to get out of this mess, mainly to avoid embarrassment. I had rudely tried to invade his privacy, walked through his home without invitation, lost my temper, cussed at him, slammed his door, and then crashed my motorcycle. Sometimes I wished I was in another profession, especially when the facts didn't add up to my liking. In this case, the math was pretty clear. I was the asshole.

The cops informed me that after I was carted away in the ambulance, Big Lou had offered to take care of my bike for me. So Sunday after the group left for their ride, I decided to face my shameful self-pity and drive over to Big Lou's place, apologize and check on my bike.

I drove my truck down his gravel drive and parked it by the shed. I figured he probably had it stored in there and would just as soon have me haul it away while I was there. I limped over to the shed, but he wasn't there, so I limped to the house. I was about to knock on the front door when it opened and he said calmly, "Come in." In the middle of his living room was my motorcycle. The tank was off, but otherwise it looked fine. In fact, it looked better than it had for a long time.

"Had to repaint the tank," he said. "Replaced the left side mirror, grip, and clutch lever; otherwise the dings buffed out fine. Tank should be dry tomorrow and she'll be ready to ride."

"I'm sorry," I said. "I was out of line. I was rude and I was stupid and I'm sorry."

"I-I-I," he responded, shaking his head.

"Hey, I'm trying to apologize here," I replied.

"Don't mean nothin' to me, punk. Why's it important to you?" he asked.

"Because I screwed up," I said.

"Why?" he asked.

"I don't know," I said.

"Could it be because I-I-I?" he responded.

"Damn it!" I said. "Will you quit making me feel like shit?"

"Can someone else make ya feel like shit without yer permission?"

"Yeah, they can—and you are," I responded.

"How?" he asked.

"By calling me a punk and treating me like shit," I said.

"Why would ya care about that?" he asked.

"I want you to respect me or you won't let me lead the group," I said.

"Does respect come from what ya want or what ya give?" he asked.

I understood his point. I had been rude and disrespectful to him, yet he fixed my bike. Instead of thanking him, I had arrived with the sole objective of gaining his approval by way of a shallow apology that would make me feel better. He didn't care. Even then, while I was getting pissed off all over again, he continued to work on my motorcycle. It didn't matter to him what I thought about him, he was focused on the task at hand. What I couldn't understand was how he could be so detached. Why wasn't my apology important to him? Why didn't he care what I thought of him? More importantly, why did I care so much what he thought of me?

"Why do you keep calling me a punk?" I asked again, more rationally this time.

"I'm an asshole," he said. "Why would ya care what I called ya?"

His comment surprised me, but it also gave me my first opportunity to take the offensive. "You're right. You are an asshole, and I don't care what you think of me."

"If it don't mean nothin' to ya, there ain't no reason ta waste my time callin' ya punk."

I understood the message, but couldn't believe he really didn't care what other people thought of him. So

I decided to stay on offense.

"You're still an asshole," I said.

With my words he stood up and got right in my face. I thought he was about to explode on me, but instead he smiled and calmly and casually said, "Your ride's lookin' good. Come by and pick her up tomorrow," and walked into the kitchen. I was surprised by his reaction. I had taken a verbal shot at him, but instead of firing back, he had completely disarmed me by shifting the focus back to my motorcycle. He gave no clue how or what he felt personally.

I didn't follow him this time, but said, "I'll be by tomorrow afternoon." There was no response, so I limped back to my truck and headed home to think and do some more research. I was feeling a little depressed. Why did this old man always make me feel inferior, and why did I care?

4

Going Downhill Fast

When I got home I had a call from "Jimmy," one of the riders in our group. She wanted me to know that there had been an accident during the run that day and she was now, like me, one of the group's walking wounded. Jimmy's real name was Carol Craft. She was 34 years old and an Assistant Professor of Education at our local Texas Tech campus. She was relatively new to the group—new to riding—and she rode a Harley Sportster.

I had met her before she started riding, and although older than me, she and I got along real well. She was a great person, very intelligent and yet down to earth. Unfortunately, she had a big nose. I mean really big. One day someone compared her to Jimmy Durante, not realizing she was nearby. She overheard the comment, laughed, and did a perfect impression of him and that was it. From that point on she was forever known to us as "Jimmy." That's another thing about our group. Your name could change in a heartbeat, as long as it wasn't your idea.

I wasn't familiar with the Durante guy and had to look him up on my computer, but she clearly was. They wanted me to present her with the rocker, but I refused. I thought it would be too embarrassing. But it didn't bother Mad Dog one bit so he presented it to her. She loved it and immediately started wearing it on the back of her jacket.

I was always amazed with how she managed to

find humor in everyone and everything, especially herself. Her husband rode with us, too, and laughed right along with her. He managed a hunting ranch just east of town and had been one of the first riders in the group. She said she started riding because of him, claiming it was the only way to save their marriage. He always said her motorcycle was her way of cheating. "She'd rather ride that Harley than me," he would say. Of course, they would both laugh when he said it.

Jimmy told me the group was headed back from the Shade Tree Saloon in Spring Branch, just north of San Antonio on Highway 281. It's a regional hangout and a good place to meet riders from all over this part of the state. And in my opinion they have the best jalapeño burger in the world.

Anyway, on the way back they decided to cut over to I-10 and take the fast route home. They were on I-10 when Jimmy's husband's motorcycle started to spit and sputter just as they crested a hill that was littered with warning signs indicating road construction ahead. To complicate things further, he was the Road Captain for the ride. So when he started to slow down some people thought it was because of road construction. Since he had an emergency he pulled onto the left shoulder.

Instead of taking over the lead, the assistant Road Captain followed him, so everyone else did, too. The people in the back couldn't tell what the hell was going on, but they knew they were now just over a hill and stopped on the highway as cars and trucks sped by in the right lane at eighty miles an hour. A truck came to the crest of the hill, in their lane, and when he saw the mass confusion, he hit his brakes hard. Luckily, he stopped before he reached the group. However,

Jimmy was bringing up the rear so when she heard the screaming tires and saw that truck filling up her rear-view mirror she decided to get the hell out of there. Unfortunately, everyone else had the same idea only a few seconds later. So just as she was taking off another rider let out his clutch and slammed into her. "Bike's okay," she said. "He hit my leg and broke my ankle. Hurt like hell riding home, but I made it."

"You didn't call an ambulance?" I asked.

"Nah," she said. "It wasn't stickin' out or anything, and we were only about thirty miles from home. I just reached down and speed shifted with my hand."

"You could have been killed," I said, stating the obvious.

"Yeah, I know," she said. "The old man and I were just talking about that. You need to get better and help the group. He isn't going to do it anymore."

My heart sank and stayed that way long after our conversation ended. Jimmy's husband was one of our best riders. His riding name was "Ace" because he was the only one in our group who had taken every riding course offered by a motorcycle school in San Antonio and aced them all. He was the one who taught me what I knew about being a Road Captain. If he was worried about leading the group, why wasn't I concerned?

More Trouble at Work

When I went into work on Monday morning I had a confidential, urgent e-mail from my boss. That was never a good sign. It read simply, "See me ASAP."

My boss's name was Stanley Markley. He celebrated his fifty-first birthday the week I joined the company, just over two years earlier. He was a pleasant guy, but, I thought, a little lazy as a boss. He was quick to delegate but rarely followed up to see how we were doing. We reporters got in the habit of sharing our stories with one another because we were convinced he didn't bother to read anything we wrote before it was published. He was usually drinking coffee or outside satisfying his three-packs-a-day habit. His claim to fame, if you could call it that, was that he spent five years as an editor for the *San Angelo Standard-Times.*

The talk was he drank himself out of that job, but the only clue I had ever noticed was an old token he had framed on his office wall. It was similar to one hanging in the publisher's office, which another reporter told me was some kind of award from Alcoholics Anonymous. My boss was clearly in the twilight of his career, yet he managed to command a fairly powerful presence, at least with a young reporter like me. Although the publisher personally hired me (one of his ex-wives was my English teacher in high school), my boss didn't openly resist having me dumped in his lap. However, the first assignment he gave me was to build a web site. At the time, technology was a threat and so the task was like asking me to invite the enemy into the office. I always thought he was betting I would fail and it would give him an excuse to get rid of me.

I struggled to his office, trying hard not to show any signs of my injuries.

"Feeling okay?" he asked as I walked into his doorless office.

"Yeah, I'm fine," I said, lying as bravely as I could.

"Sorry to hear about your accident," he said.

"I was sorry to be in it," I replied, like a smart-ass, recognizing this small talk was a sign of real trouble ahead.

"We had to resolve the problem we discussed last week," he said.

"Really?" I said. "How?"

"We told them we fired you and you will be out of here in two weeks."

"So does that mean I'm fired?" I asked, feeling a growing agitation in my gut.

"If we don't find another way to resolve this, your last day is two weeks from last Wednesday. Sorry."

"Sorry?" I said. "I spend two years of my life working here…" My blood was beginning to boil with every word. "I stay up all night to meet your deadlines. I take all the shit assignments without complaint. You tell me to report as I see it then fire me because I won't kiss an advertiser's ass, and all you can say is you're sorry?"

"That's the problem," he said, getting red in the face. "It's always I-I-I with you."

I was stunned. These were the exact same words Big Lou had said to me. *Was the world going nuts*? I wondered. *Was I going nuts*?

"What the hell do you mean?" I said, more begging for information than demanding an answer.

"I mean we are a team here. We can't function unless everyone gives a little. That's just the nature of things. The reality is you say you want to be on the team, but you think you only need to do what you want. It doesn't work that way."

"So you think I should give up my principles and let the advertisers tell me what to write?" I asked, my thoughts bouncing between what he was saying and Big Lou.

"No," he said. "You really don't get it, do you? No one has asked you to compromise your principles. No one suggested you or the advertiser was right or wrong. But instead of looking at it as a business problem, you made it personal. You let your ego overrun your brain and imagined there was some kind of conspiracy against you. You made no effort to understand anyone else's point of view or show any concern for the business. By doing nothing, you threw the entire team under the bus."

My hip and leg began to ache as though signaling me my blood pressure was about to redline.

"Look," I responded in my best injured voice, "I didn't mean to ignore the problem. I was in a motorcycle accident."

"Excuses aren't going to help, not even good ones," he said. "Go home and think on it. You are a good reporter, but that's not enough. If you aren't willing to put the interests of the team first, you don't belong here. You have ten days to decide."

With those words, he stood up and turned his back to look out the window. The meeting was over.

The emotions that were erupting in my gut suddenly made me feel sick. I liked my job, but was in no position to defend it at the moment, so I left quietly. When I got to my desk, I glanced at its mess and kept going, limping more now because pretending I was not in pain no longer mattered.

When I arrived at my truck, instead of getting in and driving home I kept on walking. It was almost noon when I realized my sick feeling had been pushed aside by hunger pangs. I had been wandering aimlessly for hours and thinking so deeply that when I finally started to become aware of the world around me it took a while to recognize where I was.

Unlikely Friends

I found myself across the street from Isaack's Restaurant. So I headed over there for lunch. My hip and leg were killing me, and I was tired and hungry, so the fact that a familiar motorcycle and a police car were parked out front didn't make much of an impression on me.

As I entered, I saw Big Lou, Sheriff Gonzalez and Hangman in the back corner. Big Lou, who had his back to the wall, was looking straight at me. I hesitated at the door and looked around, acting as if I hadn't seen them. The restaurant had a buffet set up so I went straight there and fixed a plate. When I looked back in their direction with tray in hand, Big Lou motioned for me to come over. I was in no mood for their bullshit, but decided not to be rude.

As I approached, the sheriff and Hangman got up. The sheriff greeted me with, "How are you, young man?"

"Fine, sir," I responded.

Hangman said, "Be careful of the jalapeño beans today, kid. They could produce a rumor hot enough to burn the whole town down." Then he started laughing.

Sheriff Gonzales said, "Judge, have you been sharin' your old philosophy about rumors again?"

"Yes sir," I said. "He explained it to me just the other day."

Hangman and the sheriff were both about to say something when Big Lou spoke up. "Don't be messin' with my probate," he said to them, then turned to me and asked, "Or are you here to do some reportin'?"

I didn't know for sure what he meant when he referred to me as his probate, but I was still focused on the fact that I had just lost my job. "I think I just got fired."

I saw Big Lou, Hangman and the sheriff look at each other. Then Big Lou looked at me and said, "What do ya mean ya think? Did ya or didn't ya? Sit down," he commanded. The other two excused themselves and left.

"It's a little complicated," I said.

"Ya have a real talent for making things complicated," he said. "Do ya have shit on yer boots or not?"

I ignored him while I thought about a response. He waited patiently. I decided to give him a few details to see if he had any advice.

"They told me I wasn't a team player because I refused to violate my principles."

"If ya think they're assholes, why did ya work there?" he asked.

"I wrote an article that pissed off an advertiser." I was starting to download in an attempt to avoid answering his question. "My editors called me in and told me there was a problem and asked me what I planned to do about it. I figured they wanted me to write a retraction or contact the advertiser and apologize, so I left and didn't do anything. Then I got into my accident. I show up this morning and they tell me I need to decide if I'm going to do what they want, quit or be fired."

"What do they want ya to do?"

"They want me to fix the problem."

"What problem?"

"The pissed-off advertiser."

"Why is the advertiser pissed off?"

I thought about that question for a few seconds and

realized I didn't know for sure what it was about my article that made the CEO mad. Damn it! I had violated all my own rules as a reporter. I was jumping to conclusions without bothering to gather the facts.

My head dropped and I meekly said, "I don't know."

"Mmmm..."

I interrupted, "I'm a real self-centered asshole, aren't I?"

"Yep," he agreed, adding, "Aren't we all?"

"Hey, man," I said, "I was looking for sympathy. Quit raggin' on me."

Then it struck me. I understood his point. I had spent my short career as a reporter sifting through people's various points of view, egos, personal agendas and the like, all in hopes of discovering facts and "the truth." I just never thought about it in the context of my own life. My mind kept jumping back and forth between my problems at work and Big Lou. Could they be coming from the same source? Is that why Fingers was always calling the group a hopeless bunch of lone wolves? Because we focused on ourselves, not the group?

I started thinking about what I had read about group dynamics and mumbling out loud again. "The nature of groups is that people must give up some individualism to participate. But that's contrary to our instinct for self-interest. It's like a tire and the road. Without traction there is no control."

"How do ya get traction when yer world's full a bullshit?" he said, breaking into my conversation with myself.

"I think..." And he interrupted me again.

"Ya plan to think the shit off yer boots?" he said sarcastically.

He waited patiently, his eyes fixed on me. Finally, I said, "It's communication, isn't it? 'The only hope I have of saving my job is to talk with the advertiser and get the facts straight. Communication is what gives people the traction needed to work together or live together... shit... or ride together. That's it, isn't it? That's what you've been trying to tell me."

He just shook his head and said, "I asked if ya had shit on yer boots and yer telling me about the grass the cows ate. What the hell's goin' on in that shit pile ya call a brain?"

"Okay", I said, "I get it. I'm over-thinking the obvious. I'm sorry, but I have never thought about this stuff before."

"It's hard to see the world when yer head's so far up yer own ass, isn't it? Have ya ever tried changing the view?" he said with a smile.

It made me remember my conversation with Fingers and what MCs think about riders with their heads up their own ass. *Was that me*? I wondered.

Just then Big Lou said, "Ain't that complicated. When ya got shit on yer boots there ain't but four choices. Wipe em' clean, kick hard, lick em' and eat shit or wait for the rain. Ya need to decide, then don't think no more, just do it. Nobody else will give a damn, long as it ain't their boots and they can't smell yours. They won't even care if it's their shit ya stepped in. Time for me to ride," he added, getting up to leave. "Yer bike is ready whenever you are."

It was the first time I remembered him saying anything to me that even came close to a joke. Despite the fact that he had once again cut me to the core, I understood he wasn't trying to hurt me. I actually felt better than I had when I walked in the door. I knew what I had to do. He made sure of that before he rode off.

I decided to walk back to my truck and head home, change into my riding clothes and pick up my motorcycle. I'd worry about my job tomorrow. Right now I needed to figure out how to get my head out of my ass.

Learning the Rules

The walk back took about thirty minutes and gave me time to think about everything without the emotions that controlled me earlier in the day. As a reporter and a motorcycle rider, I had always considered myself an individualist. In fact, I took pride in being independent, doing my own thing. I resisted anytime I thought anyone was trying to take that away from me. I resisted my boss. I resisted Big Lou. Now I was beginning to realize Big Lou, for one, wasn't trying to take anything from me. He was trying to help me navigate situations that naturally required a piece of my independence. I couldn't have it both ways, but I didn't want to listen. I had thought of myself as being on the road to success and a good communicator, yet it was becoming clear I still had a lot to learn.

When I arrived home to change into my riding clothes, I checked for a collared motorcycle shirt. No luck. All I had for riding were T-shirts so I made a mental note to buy a riding shirt with a collar. I don't know why—maybe I hoped it would make me more like Big Lou. I had decided to walk the mile to his place and ride home. As I was walking I called the office to get the number for the advertiser. I called the guy and left a message with his secretary, making note of the date and time of the call on the notepad I always carried in my back pocket. (It would be a few years before I got a PDA.)

As I continued walking I mentally switched off my

trouble at work to think about Big Lou. I decided it was time for me to learn more about the guy. I put him at about forty when he arrived in town, so he must have been over fifty now. Yet he appeared full of energy and never paused to search for words when he spoke like most old guys. He never owned a car that I knew of and had only two motorcycles that I had seen—the one he rode and the one in his living room. I wasn't sure how old his ride was, but it wasn't new. Even so, it looked like it just came off the showroom floor. It had a Harley frame with a pan head motor, but other than that I couldn't tell what kind it was.

I had never seen him ride with anyone else or attend any of the charity rides my group participated in. He didn't appear to have a job, yet there was nothing in his living room to hint at any interest besides motorcycles. Still, I was starting to think he was the smartest person I had ever met. He was a mystery.

By the time I reached his gravel driveway, I had managed to think myself into being excited. I had a whole list of questions ready when I knocked on the door. There was no answer. I knocked again. Nothing. So I walked over to the shed. He wasn't there. I decided to go in and look around, thinking maybe I could find something in there that would help me figure him out. When I entered, I remembered to take off my sunglasses, and my eyes adjusted quickly. The last time I was in the shed I hadn't noticed all the motorcycle parts or the two dirt bikes back in the far corner. They looked very clean. I estimated there were enough parts to build at least three more rides. Everything looked surprisingly organized and orderly. *Strange,* I thought. Just like his house, the outside of the shed appeared to be old and worn, but on the inside it was immaculate.

Just then, he came roaring down the driveway and into the shed.

He got off his motorcycle and immediately said, "Is there a reason ya disrespect other people's space?"

I was embarrassed. "I'm sorry," I said. "I shouldn't be in here uninvited. I was waiting for you to get home and just passing the time. I didn't mean any disrespect."

"Should I listen to what ya say or to what I see?" he asked.

"I understand your point," I said, feeling a little irritated. "I was really looking forward to seeing you, and I just wasn't thinking."

He came around directly in front of me, looked me straight in the eye and said, "Bullshit." Then he stood there staring at me, as though daring me to respond. He was in my face. He was in my space. He was challenging me, and I wasn't sure what to do or what he would do.

At that point the past few days flashed through my mind, and then it struck me: *This old bastard is doing this on purpose. He's trying to see how I will react.* He was fishing and wanted to see if I would take the bait.

"I'm sorry you feel that way," I said calmly, resisting my instinct to verbally attack. "I shouldn't have come in here uninvited, but I was hoping I would find something that would help me learn more about you. I would really like to get to know you better. If I've offended you I apologize and will leave right now. I just need my bike." I struggled to keep my gaze strong and directed into his eyes as I spoke.

He was still—for an abnormally long time, considering his usual quick responses. Finally he took a step back and said, "Much better. Yer motorcycle's in the parking lot next door. Key is in the kitchen."

I had been so focused when I arrived I failed to notice it parked in my usual spot.

"I must have walked right by it when I arrived," I thought out loud.

"Thinkin' too much?" he asked.

"Yeah," I admitted. "I really would like to know more about you," I added.

"Key is on the kitchen table," he replied. "Go on in and get it. I've got stuff to do out here."

It was obvious he had no intention of letting his guard down, so I went to the house. Not wanting to add fuel to the fire, I went straight to the kitchen and picked up the key, which was the only thing on the table. I noted there was a frame on the kitchen wall. It was the first thing I had seen that revealed any hint of personality. The frame held a feather with some sort of note below. I decided not to take the time to read it and retreated from the house as quickly as I could.

I went back to the shed to let him know I had not lingered in his home and to ask him about something that had just occurred to me.

"So, why did you put my motorcycle next door?" I asked. "Were you afraid someone would think you had a visitor?" Maybe taking the offense would get me a little more information.

"You like to ride on gravel?" he asked.

Damn it, I thought. *How did he know*?

I had parked next door, partly because I was intimidated on my first visit and partly because I don't like riding a street bike on loose gravel. I had envisioned myself driving down his driveway, slipping and dumping. It wasn't the kind of entrance I imagined would help my prospects of getting through this mess.

But I wasn't going to give in now.

"I prefer pavement, but gravel doesn't bother me," I responded. *Not much of a lie,* I thought.

"Bullshit," he said instantly. Then looking at me intently he added, "Ya said ya wanted to be a Road Captain, so here is the last question I may ever ask ya. Which is more dangerous, especially to a group stupid enough to follow you, gravel or bullshit?"

He had me cold and I knew it. I had come to him a little nervous, but arrogant enough to think he would give me a few pointers and send me on my way. Instead he exposed my self-doubt and selfishness, cut my knowledge of people to the core, taught me the importance of clear communication and proved that my skills sucked. I was alternating between feeling pissed off and feeling completely incompetent. But to my surprise I didn't think about quitting or finding anyone or anything to blame—habits I was beginning to see in myself that I didn't like. I had promised myself I was not going to give up. I was going to do whatever it took to prove myself to this old man, even if it meant pushing aside my ego.

"Will you teach me what I need to know to become a Road Captain? I'll do whatever you ask of me."

"You've already been voted most popular, haven't ya?"

He had already made me feel completely incompetent and now he was telling me the members of my group didn't know what they were doing. He was right, of course.

"Yes, but I'm not qualified," I responded.

For the next hour we sat on stools next to his workbench and talked about motorcycles, leadership, people and me. He surprised me with his passionate thoughts about riders. "Outlaws are outlaws," he said. "Motorcycles got nothin' to do with it. Bad don't come from the machine. It comes from here," he said, pointing at my heart. "Put a bad heart in a tie and fancy car and the result's the same.

"Motorcycles don't make ya free neither. If ya ain't free when ya saddle up ya won't be free when ya get off. Freedom comes from here," he said, pointing at my head. Ya ain't ridin' free when yer brain bucket's full a bullshit. Yer just runnin' away," he said.

He concluded his lesson with a brutal assessment of me and my leadership ability. "Just because there's someone in yer rearview mirror don't mean you're a leader," he said. "Some people would wait in line at the gates of hell just because there were other people around. A real leader makes sure his people know where he's headed at all times, puts their needs first and lets them choose to follow or not. The job is hard. Ya need to respect people and learn to listen to somethin' other than yer own ego. Ya need ta know who ya are.

"If ya wanna be one of them assholes that call themselves leaders, but use people for pride, power or pussy, go ahead. There's lots of opportunity, and ya would fit right in. But don't expect me ta step in yer shit cause I'm gonna be as far away from yer sorry ass as I can get."

He regarded me, but not with a challenging expression. It was more like he didn't really give a shit how I answered. He was just waiting for a response.

"I'm not interested in taking the easy road," I said.

"Are ya busy tomorrow?" he asked.

"No," I responded immediately, deciding instantly nothing was more important to me, not even saving my job.

"Meet me at the Junction for breakfast. We'll go for a ride. Plan to be gone all day." Then he turned and started working on his bike, signaling our conversation was over.

6

Learning How to Lead

Like a child anticipating Christmas morning, sleep was not a real option for me that night, so about 1:00 in the morning I decided to get up, write out my notes and do a little more research. About 4:00 a.m. I gave sleep one more try.

I drifted off, and a short time later, or at least what seemed like a short time later, I was awakened by the phone. It was my boss. The advertiser had contacted him to let him know I had called.

"He didn't return my call," I said. "I thought about our meeting, and I need some more facts before deciding what to do."

He said, "It's good you called him. Let me know how it goes when you make contact."

I looked at my alarm clock. It was 9:00 a.m. "Shit, I gotta go," I said out loud.

There was a faint sound of "What?" from the phone as I slammed it down before getting dressed in a hurry. We had not set a time to meet, but I had planned to ride out around 7:00 a.m. just to make sure I wasn't late. *Damn it!* I thought as I was putting my boots on. *I am such an irresponsible idiot. He is going to crucify me.* But when I arrived at the Junction Restaurant, he was nowhere in sight.

I asked the waiter, who was also the cook, dishwasher and cashier at that time of day, if anyone had been there earlier.

"Lots a folk," he said.

The Junction Restaurant was right on the edge of town near the interstate, and it got some I-10 traffic, but not much. On the outside it wasn't much to look at, but the food and service were great. There were a couple of chain restaurants nearby, however, so most of their business came from locals.

"Big Lou been in?" I asked.

"Nope," he said. "Want something to eat?" Suddenly I was very hungry.

"Yeah," I said. "Bring me two egg, bacon and cheese tacos and some black coffee, please."

"I'll get 'er," he said, and off he went to get the coffee pot before putting on his chef's hat.

I had just finished eating when I heard a motorcycle. Less than a minute later in came Big Lou. He walked straight to me and said, "Mind if we move to the corner table?"

"No, I don't mind," I said, and he smiled.

"Thanks," he said. Then he walked over, took off his leather jacket and sat in the corner chair with his back to the wall.

"I thought I was late and missed you," I said. "I overslept this morning."

"How could you be late?" he asked.

"I planned to be here by 7:30. What time did you plan to be here?" I asked.

"When I got here. What time did you think?" he asked matter-of-factly.

"I didn't know, so I just planned to get here early."

"Would it have been easier if I told ya what time I planned to be here?" he asked.

"Of course," I said.

"Aren't you the Road Captain?" he asked.

"I thought you were in charge," I said.

"Mmmm... then why did ya make yer own plan? Why didn't ya ask me what time to be here?"

"Why didn't you tell me?" I responded back.

"Good question," he replied. "Why do ya think?"

I thought for almost a minute. I had gotten past taking his questions personally. Instead of responding with my ego, I was beginning to feel safely detached, like I was reporting on someone else's experience. It's hard to explain, but for the first time I felt free to think and observe. It was a good feeling.

"You did this on purpose, didn't you?" I asked.

"Did what?" he responded.

"You asked me to meet you here knowing I was too stupid to ask what time. So you show up at 10:45, which is ridiculous, to be sure I got the message."

"What's the message?" he asked.

"We had a half-assed plan, no structure or communication. We have no traction."

"That's the first time I've heard ya use the word 'we.' Ya weren't in the military, were ya," he said, more as a statement than a question.

"No," I said hesitantly.

"Didn't play team sports either," he stated.

"No, not really," I responded defensively. "I did do some sports reporting in college. How about you?" I asked, hoping to pull just a crumb of information about him.

He slid out of the booth and said, "Some military. Ready to ride?" His response surprised me. He had actually answered a personal question, which made me want to ask more. But he was already headed out the door. I followed, deciding to resist the urge to probe further, at least until our next stop.

When we got to the bikes, I asked where we were

going. "Yer the Road Captain," he said.

"Okay," I said. "How about Bandera?"

"Fine," he said.

We started the motorcycles, and I glanced over to make sure he was ready to roll. He smiled, so I took off for Bandera. I was just about to shift into second gear when I glanced in my mirror. He was still sitting in front of the restaurant. I figured he must have a problem so I did a U-turn and rode back.

"Something wrong?" I asked when I pulled up next to him.

"No, why?" he responded.

"You didn't leave with me," I said.

"Did ya want me to?" he asked.

"Of course," I said.

"Ya think I'm an idiot?"

"Why would you say that?"

"Who else would follow you?"

I was quickly losing my detached view of this experience and could feel the eruption beginning in my gut. Out of desperation I said, "We agreed I would be the Road Captain, so what the hell's the problem?"

"What's the Road Captain's job?" he asked.

"To lead the ride," I responded.

"Who besides an idiot follows a leader without a plan? I figured ya must think I'm an idiot," he said, shrugging matter-of-factly.

"We agreed we were going to Bandera," I said. But before the words were out of my mouth, I understood what he was getting at. There were at least three different routes we could take to get to our destination. The only plan I had was ride to Bandera as I always had, taking whatever route struck me as I was riding. I was not thinking about leading a ride. I was just thinking about my own ride, assuming he would be in my mirrors following blindly along. He had just finished teaching me the problems half-assed plans create, and already I was acting like I hadn't learned a thing. The problem was I didn't know what to do next.

"I'd like you to teach me how to lead a ride," I said. I understand your point, but I don't know what to do."

"Still want to go to Bandera?" he asked as he dismounted his motorcycle, reached into a saddlebag and pulled out a map.

"Yeah," I said.

He opened the map and pointed out a route, suggesting we take Highway 377 to Road 41, then Road 336 to Leaky, then Road 337 to Medina, and Highway 16 into Bandera. It was a great route that would take us across two of the three Twisted Sisters, a famous Texas motorcycle route that I sometimes took for granted. He asked me my opinion at every turn.

Once the route was established, he said, "Want to ride peg to peg, nose to tail, or staggered?"

In case you don't know, peg to peg is riding side by side, nose to tail is one behind the other and staggered uses the right and left positions in a lane. I had always imagined riding peg to peg with Big Lou. It's just the way I figured the old guy rode. But I wasn't really comfortable with the idea, because there was less of a margin for error. So risking what he would think of me, I said, "Staggered."

He said, "Good answer. On my right one second behind, okay?"

I was pretty sure I knew what he meant. The staggered formation was the way my group rode. We rarely discussed intervals, but I knew the standard was one second between the lead bike in the left lane position and the second bike, which was in the right lane position. The third motorcycle was directly behind the lead and two seconds back. I had no idea where the formation came from or why, so I thought I'd better check.

"If you mean using three lane positions with you riding on the left as the lead bike, the center is open and I'm one second behind you in the right portion of the lane, yeah."

He just smiled and said, "Use hand signals before?"

"Yeah," I said.

"Show me," he said, and I showed him the hand signals my group sometimes used to communicate with one another while riding.

"Okay, that's what we'll use. Come up on the right or put on yer flashers if ya need my attention. Repeat my signals so I know they were received. Speed preference?" he asked.

"No," I said. "Although I prefer not to see the sheriff or Hangman today."

He laughed and said, "Questions?"

"What branch of the military were you in?"

"You ready to roll?" he asked, ignoring my question.

I nodded.

"Army," he said, mounting his motorcycle and starting it.

He looked over at me, and I gave him the thumbs up. He motioned and started to roll. *Army*, I thought as I pulled out behind him and fell into position.

My First Real Ride

It quickly occurred to me that I was riding with Big Lou. Over the years I had heard a lot of stories, but this was real. Despite his legend and my sleepless night anticipating this moment, I didn't feel apprehensive at all. I admired the simple yet confident way he took charge before we left and appreciated how he made me feel part of the ride. No bullshit, no jokes, no brain twisters, just business. This would not be my ride or his ride; it was *our* ride. *Way cool,* I thought to myself.

As we twisted up and down the hilly roads on our route, he never made a move without signaling me or did anything without creating enough room for me to easily follow along. I had never felt like this riding with my group. I decided it was because we didn't have real leadership. Just people like me. "Or like I used to be," I said to myself, pledging again to become a real Road Captain.

Watching Big Lou ride was beautiful. He and his machine were one as they flowed down the road. Their movements were so natural, smooth and steady that maintaining my position was not only easy, it was fun. Following him took the edge off the sharp turns, switchbacks and hills. The rush was still there, but it was easier to know the correct speed and which line to take through corners.

We had ridden about fifty miles when I lost my concentration for a second. He entered a corner faster than I felt comfortable because I was late making my press and lean to negotiate the curve, so I backed off. For those of you who don't know, you don't just steer a motorcycle around a corner like a car. With two wheels it's necessary to lean in the direction you want to go, or the machine will keep going straight and run off the road. When I came out of the corner, I realized he had let up on his throttle so it would be easier for me to catch up. I was embarrassed.

Damn it, I thought. *He probably thinks I'm a wimp.* Without thinking, I hit the throttle and pulled up next to him, revving my engine and jumping forward, inviting him to race. He motioned for me to go ahead, and I took off diving into the next corner faster than I had ever ridden it before. Adrenalin was taking over so I kept going, diving into another corner. I was doing it. I was showing him I was no wimp. I was showing him I knew how to ride. I felt a sense of pride as I looked in my mirror to see where he was. But he wasn't there, so I pulled over and waited. One minute passed, then two. *Shit,* I thought, *maybe he missed a corner trying to follow me. I was going pretty fast.* So I turned around and raced back to find him. But Big Lou was not on the side of the road. He was nowhere in sight. He was gone.

7

Learning About the Legend

I retraced our route back to town and saw his motorcycle outside the Wild Turkey Saloon. I couldn't imagine what was going on. Why would he just leave me? Until that moment I had been enjoying the best ride of my life. More out of curiosity than courage, I decided to go in and demand some answers.

When I walked in he was sitting at the end of the bar with his back to the wall. He looked at me and smiled.

"Glad to see ya made it back," he said.

As hard as I tried, I could not hold back. "What the hell is wrong with you?" I demanded. "I'm on the best ride of my life and you just leave me? What's up with that?"

"Did I leave you or did ya run off ahead to count coup?"

Junction was once Indian Territory—and I had also taken a course on North American Indian culture in college—so I understood the reference. He was accusing me of running off ahead to prove myself.

"I thought we were going to race," I said.

"Was that our plan?" he asked.

I had no choice but to admit we had not discussed racing, but it happened a lot in my group. It wasn't unusual for someone to challenge another rider until soon we were all competing against one another as we made our way down the road. Occasionally, someone in the group complained about it, but it didn't change things. We figured it was the normal, unavoidable result of combining our competitive natures and adrenalin. Apparently Big Lou didn't agree.

"No, I just felt like doing it," I said.

"So ya felt like ignoring the plan and takin' over leadership while we were rollin' down the road. Why would I ride with someone who don't give a shit if I live or die as long as they get to do what they feel like doin'?"

"I wasn't thinking that way," I said.

With that he grabbed my shirt and pulled my face close to his. "Ain't it time ya quit pretendin' to be a warrior!"

"What the hell does that mean?" I said, pulling back but being careful to avoid breaking eye contact. He suddenly looked sad and tired, as though the energy were draining from his body. I thought I saw a tear well up in one eye and could tell he was thinking very deeply.

"How can I help ya become something ya can't see?" he said, speaking more to himself than to me.

"Are you okay, Lou?" I asked.

"Look, kid," he said, "if ya wanna kill yourself, go ahead, I can't stop ya, but don't pretend ya care about me or anyone besides yer self. I'm tired. Go home and let me be." He turned away to signal an end to our conversation.

I decided it was best to heed his advice.

More Research

As soon as I got to my bike I remembered my cell phone. It was in my backpack and completely forgotten. I had not checked messages all day. I decided it could wait until I got home. I didn't want to talk to anyone at the moment.

On the short ride home I found myself worrying about Big Lou. It was like I had said or done something that flipped a switch. His whole personality, even his expression, changed. I went over the day and our conversations again and again. I knew I screwed up but didn't think anything I had done was that serious. He obviously thought differently. I decided to do a little online research on the "warrior" thing. Maybe I could find a clue about what was going on in his mind.

By the time I got home it was a little after 2:00 in the afternoon and I had six messages. Two were from my boss, who wanted to know if I was okay because we had been cut off and he couldn't reach me on my home phone. " Stinky," one of the members of my riding group, wanted to know if I had planned a ride for the next weekend, and my mother called twice. She wanted to know if everything was all right because she hadn't heard from me since my accident.

My mother was not all that protective of me, so her calls were a little surprising. She had gotten pregnant with me when she was just nineteen. She was already on her own living in Kerrville and working at the Dairy Queen right off I-10. One day she met a motorcycle rider by the name of Mike Kountz. She told me he was headed to San Antonio and they fell in love instantly. He stayed for a week, and after he left she never saw him again. I was born nine months later. She always claimed to love three things in this world: me, motorcycles and San Antonio. We moved to San Antonio for a year after I was born and then came to Junction. I don't think she ever gave up on the idea that some day the guy would come back for her. She never married or dated anyone that I know of, just waited tables at Isaack's Restaurant and took care of me. The day I left for college, she moved back to San Antonio and is still there working at a Taipei restaurant. They are famous locally for their food and service so she makes a pretty good living. I tried to get down there once a month or so back then. She always worked the swing shift so I assumed she was getting ready for work. I decided to wait and call her in the morning.

There was also a call from the advertiser's secretary, who said she was returning my call for him. They could wait, too. I would return calls later. For the moment I needed a nap.

I fell asleep on the couch and woke up about 6:30 that evening, grabbed a couple of boiled eggs from the fridge, a coke and some snacks and sat down at my computer to do a little research. I looked up the term "warriors." There were over twenty million references on the Internet so I decided to restrict my search to "army warriors" and "warrior books." I read definitions, histories, philosophies and strategies for hours. Finally, I came across the modern army Warrior Ethos and a book called *Lost Souls at Home*. The Warrior Ethos had four parts:

1. *I will always place the mission first*
2. *I will never accept defeat*
3. *I will never quit*
4. *I will never leave a fallen comrade.*

The reviews of the book *Lost Souls at Home* promised it would provide some insight into the experience of Vietnam Veterans after returning home. I decided to pick up a copy in the morning. I still couldn't connect the dots so I continued my investigation by searching the term "Road Captain." I was shocked to find over a million references on the subject. I never thought it referred to anything other than the person riding the lead motorcycle. Now I was finding out there were Road Captain courses, papers, discussions and opinions—every detail about the job was discussed. It was even argued that a good ride involved a ride planner, a ride leader, a first bike and a last bike, along with a few others, all separate jobs. That was all interesting, but nowhere did it say anything about warriors. I finally went to bed still not knowing what Big Lou's problem was.

Stinky

On Wednesday morning I walked down to the closest thing our town had to a motorcycle clothing shop and picked up the only collared riding shirt they had in my size. Then I went over to the book store and bought a copy of *Lost Souls at Home*. When I got home I returned my mother's call and assured her I was fine. I called and left a message with "Stinky" telling him I was thinking about putting together a ride to Bandera and asked him to let me know what he thought.

Stinky (whose real name was Sam Speers) and I went to high school together. He was a good friend and very reliable, especially when it came to getting information out to our group. If he said he would do something, he got it done. He was also a pretty good businessman and was in the process of taking over his family's heating and air conditioning business, which was doing very well.

Unfortunately, just after he started riding with the group, he dropped his motorcycle at our first stop for the day. The cause of the spill was a dead skunk. Equally unfortunate was the fact that he fell on the skunk when the bike went down. He wasn't hurt, but he carried a slight skunk smell with him the rest of the day. The group, being the kind-hearted people they are, immediately had a rocker made with the name "Stinky." I think he threw it away, but it didn't matter. That's been his name ever since.

Back to Business

Next I called Mr. Dunn, the advertiser. He was the CEO of our town's largest employer. I had seen him once or twice, but for the most part he stayed in his office or on his big ranch just south of town. He didn't come to you, people went to him.

His secretary put me on hold for quite a while, then she came back on and said he was busy but would call me back. I called my boss next. He wasn't in so I left a message.

I had just finished reading three chapters of *Lost Souls at Home* when the phone rang. It was the advertiser's secretary.

"Please hold for Mr. Dunn," she said.

I had been holding for quite a while when he finally came on. "Young man," he said, getting straight to business, "your article really pissed me off."

"Which article is that?" I asked. "And what about it upset you?"

"Don't bullshit me. You know which article it was," he responded firmly.

He was right. "I am pretty sure I know which one pissed you off," I said, "but I just want to make sure. I have been pissing off a lot of people for a lot of different reasons lately."

He laughed and immediately got back to business. "Why in the hell did you say my company was planning to move to Phoenix?"

"I didn't say that. I just reported someone in your company said you were considering moving. Are you?" I asked.

"Who told you we were considering moving?" he said, avoiding the question.

"I can't tell you that," I said. "Is it true?" I asked again.

"Look, your editor said he fired you. You tell me who my leak is and I'll get you your job back."

"I can't do that," I said.

"Then we have nothing more to talk about," he said, and hung up.

I noted the date and time. About an hour later my boss called. I told him about my conversation with Mr. Dunn and his demand that I give him the name of my source.

"I won't do it," I said. "If that's what it takes to keep my job, I quit."

He said, "I wish you had called him last week. I'll get back to you," and hung up.

I read for a couple of more hours and then decided to ride over and check on Big Lou.

Doing Things Right

When I arrived at Big Lou's place, I rode down his gravel drive. He came out of the shed to watch, so I pulled up in front of him and stopped.

"HOOAH! Where's all that courage comin' from?" he said.

I dismounted and said, "What the hell you smiling at?"

He just stood there smiling, not saying a word.

"You look like you're glad to see me. I thought you gave up on me," I said.

"Then why are ya here?" he asked.

"Because I was worried about you."

He laughed and shook his head. "Still feel like racin'?" Without another word, he walked into the shed and gestured for me to follow.

We took his dirt bikes out from the corner, fueled them and headed over to the racetrack, which was just behind his house. Nobody was there, but we went in through a big hole he uncovered in the back fence.

"Insurance," he said. "Their lawyers can't blame the owners if we sneak in."

For the next two hours, he taught me about real competition and real motorcycle riding. I pushed myself and the machine hard every time we went out, in hopes of catching him. Between runs, he asked me what I was feeling. He listened carefully then recommended changes for me and my equipment and sent me out on my own to practice. He taught me how to enter and exit a corner and when to hit the throttle and how to use my brakes and where to look at different points on the track. He would watch and time me, motioning me in every couple of laps for more advice. Then he would join me on the track and test me.

I wiped out a couple of times and he didn't react at all. Once we were racing and he just kept riding. The other time he was in the pit and just stood there until I got going again then called me in and checked the bike. He never said a word. After one of our races, I complained that he must have given me the slower motorcycle. He made me switch with him. It didn't help. I never caught him. The old man was just too good.

On our last run, I was getting close to exhaustion when he slowed in front of me. I assumed he was getting tired, too. I pulled into position behind him and followed along for the final two laps. It was a strange feeling. At first I thought I was just running out of adrenaline, but then I realized it was more than that. When we were racing, he competed hard and never let up. When we stopped he became my coach, helping me learn the skills needed to win. He had showed me that competition has its place, and now he was letting me know that I was more important to him than winning. He was to me, too.

When we pulled in he just looked at me, smiled and headed back to the shed, again waving for me to follow. Back at the shed we cleaned the bikes and talked like we never had before. He let me ask questions.

"How did you learn to ride like that?" I asked.

"Got tired of fallin' off, so I asked a friend fer help. He was a good rider, a lot smarter than me and a great coach. He sure could see what I was doing wrong. All

I had ta do was listen to him, think and practice a little, and the next thing I knew I wasn't falling off as much."

"Where's your friend now?"

"Dead," he said. After a pause he switched subjects. "Whatever happened to yer job?"

I told him about my conversations that morning.

"Ya must have a lot on yer mind. No wonder ya couldn't catch me," he said, more teasing than bragging.

"I have no excuses," I said. "You are a better rider than I am, and I really appreciate the time you are taking to help me." I decided this would be a good time to press him for more information about his life.

"I understand what you meant yesterday when you told me I was pretending to be a warrior. You were a warrior, weren't you? Did you serve in Vietnam?"

"Hand me that rag," he said as he continued cleaning. I handed him the rag and he said, "What do ya think I meant?"

"I read the Army's warrior ethos last night. 'I will always place the mission first.' You meant that you think I don't have what it takes because I'm a self-centered asshole."

"I didn't say that. I just don't know what to do. How can I teach ya if ya don't have a mission?"

"I thought my mission was to become a Road Captain," I said.

"I know," he responded. "That's the problem. Becoming what ya want is not a mission, it's personal ambition. A mission is bigger than anything personal. When all ya got is personal ambition, ya ain't nothin' but an outlaw in disguise!"

He was standing now, and I could tell he wanted to say more. What he was saying was obviously important to him, so I asked him another question.

"What's your mission?"

"Come with me," he said, walking out of the shed toward the house. He didn't say anything until we got to the kitchen, where he pointed to the framed feather on the wall.

"Read that," he said.

Under the feather was a note:

This Eagle feather belonged to my son and your friend Sgt. Michael Whitehorse. Our tribe gave it to him when he first became a warrior. He asked me to keep it safe while he was in Vietnam. When he did not return, I ask the Great Spirit what to do, as I am getting old. He told me to send it to you. I am happy for Michael's feather. It will have a safe place to live.

Joseph Whitehorse

I read the note twice, mainly to give myself time to regain my composure before turning back to face Big Lou.

"Did you serve with Sergeant Whitehorse in Vietnam?"

"Yes," he said. "We were buddies in high school. We rode bicycles and motorcycles and stole cars together. Want a drink?" he asked, changing the subject. I could tell he was struggling to talk.

"Just some water would be fine," I said. "I really want to know about Sergeant Whitehorse and the feather."

"Why? I thought ya quit being a reporter."

"Hey, I'm not reporting anything to anybody," I said. "Whatever you say is just between me and you. Besides, you asked me to come in here and read it. How can I understand your point if you don't tell me the story?"

He sat down at the kitchen table and talked nonstop for over two hours. He told me about how, growing up, he and Whitehorse had been virtually inseparable. They had gotten crossways with the law, so as soon as they graduated from high school, they decided to join the Army. They went through boot camp and Advanced Infantry Training together, and then were sent to Germany, then to Fort Hood in Texas. While in Germany they both bought motorcycles and started racing at a local track. Michael was a good rider but a better coach. He coached Big Lou and helped him work on his equipment until he started winning. When they were transferred to Fort Hood they continued riding together. One day they were riding out in the Texas Hill Country when Big Lou began racing and Michael took the bait. The next thing they knew they were speeding together through corners, like they were on a racetrack. Big Lou hit some loose gravel in a turn, lost it and ended up with a broken leg.

A short time later, their unit was sent to Vietnam. Big Lou was still in a cast, so he didn't go. While in Vietnam, Michael saw a lot of combat and came home a sergeant with a Purple Heart and a Bronze Star. Michael returned to Fort Hood. In the meantime, Big Lou had received orders for Vietnam. Despite his experience there the year before, Michael immediately volunteered to join his buddy.

"I told him he was crazy," Big Lou said, "and he told me it was a warrior's job to keep his friends and family safe."

"Did he die on that tour?" I asked.

"Yes," Lou said.

"How did that make you feel?" I asked.

"Numb," he said. "I stayed in the fight until I was shot up so bad they kicked me out of the Army."

"Then what did you do?" I asked.

"I got on a motorcycle and started riding," he said.

He talked quite a bit more about his friend, then went on to tell about his war experience and his life after the military. As I listened I began to realize he was not at all like the legend we had created; he was much more worthy of the status than we could have imagined.

I had been reading about how many soldiers became alienated from themselves during the Vietnam War and have spent the rest of their lives in an endless search for their soul. I wanted to let him know I was beginning to understand and respect the depth of his life. "So you settled down here because you finally found your soul?"

"What?" he responded, shaking his head. "Found my soul? I stopped here because the rent on this house was cheap, the track is close and the sheriff's a decent guy. I just never had a reason to move on. Find my soul? Where in the hell did ya get that? Ya think I don't know who I am?"

Once again he had me completely off balance. I had been researching and giving a lot of thought to this man and his questions since we first met. I couldn't help myself. I had to know who he was.

"I've been doing a lot of thinking," I said, "because

I want to get it right."

"Get what right?" he asked.

"I respect you and I want to understand you," I said.

"Ya ain't gonna find real people in a computer, Josh. Even if ya could, how can ya understand others when ya have yer head up yer own ass?" he asked.

"I'm only twenty-four," I said. "How old were you when someone pulled your head out of your ass?"

"They started pullin' at eighteen, but it didn't pop out right away," he said with a smile.

"So there's hope for me?" I asked.

"Maybe, if ya find yer feather," he said.

"You mean I need to find a mission in life, something I think is more important than me? How do I do that?"

"Mmmm… can't help ya with that one," he said. "You'll know it when ya see it, unless yer still blinded by the bullshit that keeps pourin' outta yer head." He was smiling as he said it. Then he got up, signaling it was time for me to leave.

"Why are you wasting time on me?" I asked. Listening to him talk about his amazing life, I was beginning to regret how arrogant and disrespectful I had been. I was totally embarrassed by my actions and especially my thoughts.

"I don't waste my time," he said firmly, and walked with me in silence to my motorcycle.

I did not have a coach or any kind of father figure growing up. Never in my life had I had another man make me feel the way I felt at that moment.

As I was mounting my motorcycle I said, "Hey, I need to run over to Bandera Friday to plan a run for my group. You interested in joining me?"

"Ya plan on racin' there?" he asked.

"I promise you I will never make that mistake again and I will not ride with someone who does."

"Thanks for listenin'," he said. "Friday's good for me."

I wasn't sure if he meant listening to his story or letting him know I had learned a lesson about racing. It didn't matter. I was starting to understand what was behind this legend, and it made me feel fortunate to know him.

"See you Friday," I said. "How about the Junction Restaurant at 8:00 a.m. and plan to be gone all day?"

"The Junction at zero eight hundred hours Friday. Yes sir, Captain, I'll be there," he said with a salute.

I rode home that afternoon with the strangest sense of calm. Everything was starting to make sense to me. I needed to get home and write down my thoughts.

8

The Self Test

There was something about my time with Big Lou that was so challenging mentally I rarely thought about anything else. Being around him was almost like taking a long solo ride, in which all outside cares just melt away. When I got home I remembered that I had completely forgotten to check my cell phone for messages. I had gotten into the habit of automatically turning it off when I was around Big Lou but had yet to master the art of turning it back on. It struck me that I didn't know if he had a phone. I didn't see one in his house and had never seen him use a cell phone. I didn't know anyone who didn't have a phone—or a television, for that matter. I made a note to ask him.

I had six calls. My riding friends, Stinky, Mad Dog, Toad and Dakota, had all called to let me know they liked the idea of a ride to Bandera. I was especially pleased to hear Dakota's voice. She was the real reason I took on the job as Road Captain. I thought she would be impressed.

My boss had called twice. He'd left the first message about an hour after I had called him that morning.

He said, "We need you to be here at one o'clock for a meeting."

The second call was at 1:15, and he said, "Josh, I need you to get your ass in here now! Where the hell are you?" It was just after 5:00 p.m., and I assumed he would still be in the office. But I wanted to write down my thoughts about the time I'd spent with Big Lou while it was fresh, so I decided to blow off my boss and sat down at the computer to write. No sooner had I started than my cell phone rang. It was my boss. Despite the urge to ignore it, I picked up.

"Hey, boss," I said.

"Where the hell you been?" he said. "I had a meeting set up this afternoon to straighten everything out, and you went and disappeared."

"Sorry, boss," I said. "I had something come up. Besides, I thought you told me to take two weeks off."

"Damn you," he said. "I'm here getting beat up fighting for your job and you don't even care. Did your mother die or something? What could possibly be more important than saving your job?"

This was the guy who once told me he thought there should be a law against motorcycle riding because it was too risky. He always looked for the easy way out. That's why he agreed to fire me. I doubted he would fight for anything except saving his own ass.

"Bullshit," I said.

"What?" he asked.

"I said bullshit. You aren't getting beat up fighting for my job, you need me for something. What happened? The web site go down?"

"Damn you," he said. "What the hell's got into you? You find another job already?"

"No," I said, "but I've learned a couple things in the last few days. What is there to meet about? I told you Mr. Dunn was trying to blackmail me into giving up my source."

"Listen to me," he said. "It's not that simple."

"Sure it is," I responded. "Either you support me or you don't. If the company can't support me I have no reason to stay."

"Look, I don't know what the hell's going on with you. Come in tomorrow morning early. I need you to help me with a couple things."

"Sure," I said, "but I won't be available Friday."

"Fine," he said. "Just get your ass in here in the morning."

During my conversations with Big Lou I had started detaching myself and become more like an observer. I did it all the time as a reporter, but I was discovering I didn't use the skill in my personal life. Most of the time, I just thought about me and as a result let my ego rule my thoughts and words. That was how my boss had learned to communicate with me, and I could feel his confusion when he realized I didn't want to play that game anymore.

I spent the rest of the evening snacking on junk food, transcribing notes, researching and listening to music, mostly at the same time. I was determined to learn everything I could about being a Road Captain before my ride with Big Lou on Friday.

Back at Work

I went into the office at seven o'clock on Thursday morning. My desk looked like it always did, but for some reason the mess was bothering me. I decided it was time to clean up a little. About five minutes after 7:00, my boss called and asked me to come into his office. I told him I was cleaning my desk and asked if it could wait a few minutes. Even though he was less than 60 feet away and could see me through his big glass window, he paused as though in shock. Then he said, "Okay."

I took most of the papers on my desk and threw

them in the trash, wondering why I had kept them in the first place, since everything I did at work was now stored on my computer. I put a few notes I had made to myself and planned to transcribe in my inbox along with a couple of company memos. The publisher still liked to distribute paper memos for some reason. In all, it only took about three minutes and my entire desk was free of clutter. My first day on the job was the only other time I remembered being able to actually see my desktop.

When I finished I walked over to the editor's office. He didn't have a door so I knocked on the glass pane next to the opening where a door would be if he had one.

"Come in," he said. "What have you been up to?" He was making small talk.

"You said you had some things you needed help with?" I asked, getting right down to business.

"Yeah," he said. "I need you to fix the web site."

No shit, I thought to myself. "What's the problem?" I said.

"How the hell would I know? Your generation's the only ones who know about that crap. Just get it fixed, will you. Everybody's on my ass."

"Look," I said, "you fired me so I moved on. I'll fix the web site, but I'll need a few days to decide if I really want to work here. Can I get back to you next week?"

"Don't push me," he said, looking me straight in the eye. I didn't move and returned his stare.

"You want me to quit now or call you next week?"

He looked away and said, "Call me Monday."

"Another thing," he said. "You still ride motorcycles with Judge Houston?"

Just a few days ago I would have assured him I was

the best of friends with Hangman. But for some reason I wasn't thinking about me or pumping up my ego. I was more detached. I was thinking about the question from another point of view. It was none of his business who Hangman or I rode with.

"No, not often," I said. "Why?"

"Damn sheriff gave me a ticket this morning and told me to see the JP when he got back this afternoon," he said.

I didn't dare imagine his problem was anything other than a coincidence, but I was having trouble keeping from laughing. I did manage to say, "What was the ticket for?"

"Failure to stop," he said. "Hell, he got me pulling out of my own driveway onto the street. I didn't know you had to stop before pulling out of your own driveway."

"Guess so," I said. "Sorry, I can't help." I turned and went immediately to the men's room. My face felt like it was about to explode as I tried to hide my laughter from the rest of the staff. Once I was alone and released my emotions, I couldn't help but wonder what the sheriff was doing outside my boss's house at six o'clock on a Thursday morning. It was amusing to think I may have been the reason.

I had looked at the web site after my boss called the night before. I knew he needed something and assumed that was it. It was obviously a problem with the server so I called Toad, one of my riding friends, and he got to work on it. He ran a small computer service business and had a rack of servers that hosted most of the business web sites in town, including ours.

Toad

Manuel Hernandez was his real name. He had a wife and two young daughters, and was thirty-two or so. He was a real nice guy, smart but very quiet, and always managed to look shocked when someone in the group did something crazy or told a dirty joke. The truth is he was one of only four in our group that had a Breezy Rider patch.

The February before, a group of about twenty riders from Junction had ridden down to Boerne, Texas for the St.Valentine's Day Massacre. It's a motorcycle rally put on by the Gypsy Motorcycle Club. Anyway, everybody was sitting around a campfire talking when a rider went by on a qualifying run for a Breezy Rider patch. To earn the patch you had to ride naked in front of a bunch of witnesses. I understand that, in the interest of safety, some groups do allow you to wear your boots.

Well, Toad decided immediately he wanted one of those patches, but his wife would have no part of it. So he qualified solo. Then Dakota decided she wanted one, too. I love my mother, but I have always regretted going into San Antonio to see her that night. Fingers and Comfort were the only others in our group who had the patch. They got theirs when they lived in Houston. I am in no way sorry I missed their qualifying run.

We call Manuel "Toad" because he always carries a plastic toad in his pocket. If you asked him about it he would tell you it saved his life when he almost drowned while swimming across the Rio Grande. It was his way of making sport of the public perception of his Mexican heritage. It wasn't true, of course. He had a family history in Junction that went back about

150 years. But he sure got a kick out of telling that story. Illegal immigration was more a joke to us than a topic of serious conversation. If you needed help, nobody gave a shit who had papers and who didn't, as long as they would work for whatever you could afford to pay. I think Toad used that gimmick because people were always trying to get him to do their computer work cheap. Hangman liked the story so much he was known to bring out of town guests to our gatherings just so they could hear it. It was about the only time Toad talked and Hangman didn't.

I called Toad to see if he found the computer problem. He had. I had told him the night before not to fix it until I called, so I gave him the okay to work his magic. (There was nothing urgent about our web site in those days.) Everything was back to normal in minutes, and I decided to head over and see Big Lou.

Learning Outside the Computer Box

When I got to Big Lou's place he was in the shed but didn't come out when I pulled up. I knew he could hear my motorcycle, but he didn't acknowledge my presence, so I knocked on the sliding door and stood outside. I had the feeling I was taking another of his tests.

He looked up, smiled and said, "Come in. Thought we didn't ride till tomorrow?"

"We don't," I said. "I just have a few questions for you."

"Ya still legend-huntin', mister reporter?" he asked. "Ain't nothin' can kill a legend quicker than a reporter's questions, ya know."

"Come on, man," I said. "I'm not a reporter anymore, remember?"

"Then why'd ya go to work this morning?" he asked.

"How did you know I went to work?"*This guy is amazing,* I thought to myself. *Was someone following me? Did he have something to do with the sheriff being outside my boss's house?*

"Well, I'll be damned if ya can't defy nature with how much life can pass ya by without ya even takin' notice," he said. "I always dress to ride like I'm gonna fall off. Don't hurt as much when I do. You dress like yer goin' to the office. That hurts, don't it?"

He was right. I was not dressed to ride. I was dressed for work. That's how he knew. I was mad at myself for not figuring that out. But more important, riding in my work clothes was a bad habit I had sworn would end after my accident. Here I was still sore and already making the same mistake. I decided to kick myself in the ass later. In the meantime, I had questions I wanted to ask Big Lou.

"Sorry," I said.

"Don't think so much," he replied. "Wanna help me put this motor together?" he asked. "Ain't real dirty," he said with a touch of sarcasm.

"Sure," I said. "What do you do with all this stuff anyway?" I asked.

"I ride it," he said in a matter of fact tone.

Then he started telling me a story for everything in the shed. While he was talking he assembled the engine. He would pause with every piece to ask me what it was and how it worked. I didn't know many answers so he would tell me about each part and how to care for it. I had fixed a few tires in my day and usually changed my own oil, if I couldn't find Fingers, but this was a real education. He didn't just ride; he understood every part of the machine, even what various motorcycle gaskets were made of and how different fluids reacted depending on the manufacturer. I was completely fascinated by the level of detailed knowledge he possessed. What's more, he was clearly enjoying teaching me, and I loved every minute.

When the engine was back together, we sat there by his work bench and kept talking. I asked him a lot of questions about things I had read about riding and leading a ride. I finally got the courage to ask him about something that had been bothering me.

"Why did Hangman make me come see you?" I asked.

"He didn't make ya do anything," he said. "He just scared the shit outta ya and you did the rest," he added, and then started laughing. "Ya just didn't have the cajones to be honest with yourself." I knew *cojones* was Tex-Mex slang for balls, but I still didn't understand his point.

"What do you mean?" I said.

"You ain't that stupid. "Ya knew what Hangman told ya to do was bullshit. But ya followed right along anyway."

"He said he would take my bike," I said, trying to justify my decision.

"Some people are so afraid of gettin' snake bit they run from snakes that ain't got no teeth," he said.

I understood what he meant. I knew I hadn't violated any laws and that Hangman had no real authority to force me to do anything. I did what he told me to do because I was intimidated. It didn't matter if it was right or wrong. However, I still wasn't sure it would have been wise for me to just ignore his order. Rather than continuing to defend myself, I decided to give him the benefit of the doubt and ask a question that was more important to me.

"Okay," I said. "I get it. But what I don't understand is why me?"

"Mmmm..." he said. "That's like askin' why the sun rises each mornin' or why the bike behind ya picked up a nail and you didn't. Some things just happen. Life's too short to waste time lookin' back and worrin' about why."

I decided to try asking the question in a different way.

"Do you think I have potential to be a leader?" I asked.

"If we can get yer head outa yer ass before some outlaw shoots ya for pretendin' to be one a them or ya go to prison for leadin' a bunch a idiots on motorcycles to the gates a hell," he said with a smile.

He got up and started walking out of the shed. I joined him. As we were walking, he said casually, "Josh, life is like ridin' a motorcycle. The trick is lookin' where ya wanna go. If ya pay attention, ya can learn more about life in one day ridin' a motorcycle than a lifetime a listenin' ta fancy talkers or starin' at a computer. Just keep yer head up and quit lookin' at yer own front fender and you'll be fine. Then he added, "I'm lookin' forward to ridin' with ya tomorrow, Captain."

My heart jumped, but I wasn't sure if it was from pride or fear of failure. I decided to head home to spend more time sorting out and writing down the things Big Lou had told me. When I got home there was another message from Dakota.

Dakota

Her real name was Linda Wildey. We met shortly after she moved to Junction from Rapid City, South Dakota. I had moved back about two months before she arrived. When she first came to town she worked as a beautician, but in less than a year she took over ownership. She had more spirit than any woman I had ever known. I was fascinated with her from the moment we met. I was working at the newspaper and had been thinking about getting a new bike at some point, but as soon as she entered my life I bought one immediately.

She was my age, and despite being just five foot six she rode a Harley Road King and was as good a rider as anyone in the group. She started hanging out with us as soon as she arrived in town and was the only one in our group with an Iron Butt patch. To earn the Iron Butt you must ride 1,000 miles in twenty-four hours and have it verified by the Iron Butt Association. She said she got hers when she was seventeen. Her father woke her up about 3:00 a.m. one Saturday morning and said, "Let's go for a ride."

"We headed west, and the next thing I knew we were in Butte, Montana," she told me. "We stopped there and he called home. He told me my mother wasn't happy and wanted us back for church in the morning so we turned around and went back. We did the miles, but it only took twenty-two hours." She always made a point of adding, "It was the best ride of my life."

I rarely saw her during the week, but I was able to be around her on Sundays when our riders got together. I mentioned earlier she was the reason I took the job as Road Captain. In fact, she was also the reason I rode with the group. But as I was dialing her number, I realized that in the two years I had known her I had rarely talked to her on the phone.

We talked quite a bit when the group was together, but hardly ever did our conversations get personal. When I asked her once why she moved from Rapid City, all she said was, "Men, snow and wind, I prefer to choose when and where."

I didn't ask her to explain what she meant. Another time, after I had had a few beers, I said, "I think we should go out sometime."

She replied, "I don't like my men to think."

I didn't follow up on that comment either. I had seen her fend off every male rider in our group and dozens of unsuspecting "panting puppies," as she called men who hit on her during our travels. She was one of those women who can completely destroy a man's courage. It's not that she's mean or deceitful or manly—far from it. In addition to her heart-stopping beauty, she was completely comfortable around men. She exuded such confidence that you knew instantly she was not at all intimidated by the world men live in. What could possibly be more dangerous to male self-esteem than that? Even though I have never had trouble playing the dating game, with her I wasn't quite sure, so I opted to stick to the friendship road. I really did want to be around her, and being friends just felt safer.

When she answered her phone, my pulse picked up a little. We talked for a minute then hit a chasm in the conversation. In desperation I said, "Hey, Big Lou and I are going to do a planning run to Bandera tomorrow. Want to join us?"

"That would be great," she said. "Let me check my

calendar. Just a second."

Shit, I thought, as I lingered on hold. *What the hell did I do this time*?

She came back on and said, "I don't have any clients scheduled. Where and what time?"

"We need to meet Big Lou at the Junction… zero eight hundred hours." I had never described time that way in my life.

"That's cool. I've heard a lot about Big Lou, but I've never met him. See ya there," she said and hung up.

I was stunned. What would Big Lou think? We sure wouldn't be able to talk about personal stuff with her around, so I could forget learning more about him—or about her, for that matter. Worse, she gave me the impression she was more interested in meeting him than riding with me. Then there was the small matter of me pretending to be a Road Captain. Would he give me a break? I doubted he would. So I spent the rest of the evening going over my research and transcribed notes from our meetings. If nothing else, I was going into this ride prepared.

9

Graduation Day

I headed for bed around midnight and set my alarm clock and my cell phone alarm, just to be sure I didn't oversleep. That turned out to be an unnecessary precaution since I was wide awake at 5:00 a.m.

About 7:45, I headed for the Junction Restaurant. I arrived ten minutes early, and both Big Lou and Dakota's bikes were already parked out front. I grabbed a map from my pack and went in. They were sitting in the back corner, Big Lou with his back to the wall, of course, and Dakota with her back to the door. They appeared to be laughing. When I reached the table, Big Lou slid to the center of his side of the booth and pointed to Dakota's side.

"Good to see ya, Captain! Care to join us?" he said. Then he grabbed my hand in a traditional high five handshake and pulled me toward him to simulate a hug.

Dakota slid over to make room for me on her side, smiled and said, "Hey."

"Dakota here tells me she feels like she already knows me, because of the stories you and yer buddies tell about our rides together."

Oh, shit! Here comes, I thought. *My worst fears are about to come true. He is going to destroy my entire life.*

Then he added, "I told her not to believe that bullshit. You are the only one I will ride with. But I will make an exception for her. She knows more about

Sturgis than I do."

Sturgis is a small town in South Dakota not far from Rapid City, and it has hosted an annual motorcycle rally for over sixty years. Dakota attended every year when she was growing up.

I could have kissed Big Lou for his response. I was sure it would cost me later, but whatever the price, it was worth it. Not only did he cover for me, he welcomed Dakota. I decided the best thing to do was to change the subject while I was ahead, so I pulled out the map and started going over a proposed route.

We talked about the route over breakfast, and when we were finished eating I did my best impression of a Road Captain.

"Any questions about the route?" I asked, pulling out a checklist I had prepared late the night before. There were no questions about the route so I went down my list.

"Any questions?" I asked when I was done.

"No sir, Captain," Big Lou said.

"Got it," Dakota said with a smile.

"Okay," I said. "Big Lou, you take the lead. Dakota, you take the right side one second behind him, and I'll take the back."

Big Lou said, "Yes, sir."

Dakota said, "I have a question. I thought you were the Road Captain. Why is Big Lou in the lead?"

I said, "Big Lou usually leads when we ride together. Just because I'm planning the ride doesn't mean I need to be the lead bike. I'm still learning, and besides, he's fun to watch ride."

"Okay, Captain," she said, giving me a hug. "Let's ride."

Big Lou winked at me and smiled as he slid out of

the booth and headed for the motorcycles.

We had gone about five miles when Dakota pulled over. She had forgotten to close her saddlebag, and it was flapping in the wind. I pulled in behind her, and Big Lou stopped just ahead and ran back.

"Both of ya put yer damn emergency blinkers on. Now!" he said. We complied immediately. Then he grabbed my shoulder and turned me around to face oncoming traffic. "Yer job is to secure the area," he said, quietly enough so Dakota wouldn't hear.

The rest of the ride to Bandera was great. We took Road 336, the east part of the Twisted Sisters, to Leakey and stopped to plan a stop for the group ride. Then we proceeded on Road 337 and twisted and turned our way to Medina, where we caught Highway 16 and rode into Bandera. Big Lou and his machine put on a show as they flowed effortlessly together through corner after corner. Traveling as one, it was impossible to tell the motorcycle from the rider. When we reached the point at which I had tried to race a few days before, I felt a twinge of embarrassment. I knew I would never make that mistake again. By then our little group had discovered a rhythm and was moving as though we were tied together. It gave me a rush. It was different than the rush I felt while racing; more like I imagined the feeling that came from being on a winning team.

When we pulled into Tequila Rita's Cantina in Bandera, I felt a little disappointed about having reached our destination. I was concerned about what Dakota was thinking, since our group had never made this long a trip with only one stop. But that concern faded quickly.

"What the hell did we stop for?" she said with a big grin.

"Cool, huh?" I said as I watched her walk over to Big Lou and throw her arms around him.

"You are beautiful," she said to Big Lou. "I have never felt that good on a group ride ever, and I have never seen anyone ride like you. Thank you for letting me ride with you."

Big Lou looked a little surprised, but true to his nature he recovered quickly. "Why don't ya plant one on the Captain?" he asked. "He did most a the work." With that she turned and gave me a hug and a kiss on the cheek. "You did great, too."

"Let's get something to drink," I said, partly to cover up my discomfort.

Tequila Rita's was a popular weekend hangout for riders, and I was happy to see several other bikes there on a Friday. It meant someone was going to see me walk in with Dakota and Big Lou. Among males there are perks for being seen with women like Dakota. It usually comes in a fleeting look of envy or a glance that lets you know that, for that moment, you are respected. But hangin' with Big Lou, well, he was a living legend. If you were seen with him you became part of his story. I figured it was the next best thing to being a legend yourself.

Dakota and I ran into a couple of friends at the cantina. Of course, everyone knew who Big Lou was, but once we were seated in the corner booth, not one person stopped to say, "Hi." They just watched us, and it felt a little strange, almost uncomfortable. It was like we were movie stars and it was okay to stare. We had a drink and discussed the ride. Then Dakota turned to Big Lou.

"Why don't you ever ride with our group?"

I was surprised that he answered without hesitation.

He normally came back at me with yet another question.

"You got no discipline," he said. "Ya'll look like Congress on motorcycles goin' down the road, and politics ain't worth dyin' for."

"I know," she said. "It does get embarrassing sometimes. But what can we do about it?"

"You just need someone worth followin'," he said.

"That would be you," Dakota said, squeezing my leg. Then she added, "Let me out, Josh. I have to pee."

Did she grab my leg because she believed I was someone worth following? Or was she talking to Big Lou and just wanted me to get out of the way so she could go pee? I couldn't tell.

As soon as Dakota went to the restroom I said, "Why do you always answer my questions with a question and yet with her you're a straight talker?"

"She has a clear mind. She knows what she knows. Yer brain's clogged with bullshit. Ya don't know what ya know. I'm tryin' to help ya do a little cleanin'," he said, pointing at my head and smiling.

"By the way," he said, "I talked to Hangman. Ya probably better go see him before yer ride Sunday. He's a little upset ya didn't ask him to come along today."

'Damn it," I said. "I forgot all about that fat old bastard." Then, remembering our conversation of the day before, I said, "I don't need his permission to lead shit."

Big Lou scowled and said, "Always know the difference between yer friends and yer enemies, Josh. And respect em' both. Either one can make ya want to twist yer throttle too hard or take yer eyes off the road. Ain't no reason for ya to disrespect Hangman. Even if yer dumb enough to think he's your enemy. He's just different. Ya disrespect everyone who's different and there won't be nobody left to lead come Sunday."

"You're right," I said.

"Ya don't need his permission to do anything. Just do yourself a favor and make sure ya invite him to join ya Sunday. It'll make him feel important."

"Invite who to join us Sunday?" Dakota asked as she returned.

"Big Lou wants to make sure Hangman knows about the ride," I said.

"Great," she said. "Want me to call him? I just love that guy. He is hilarious."

"I need to see him anyway," I said. "I'll take care of it."

Big Lou was looking at Dakota with a big grin on his face. Then he looked over at me and nodded his head in her direction. I decided it was time to get out of there before those two started another conversation, so I said, "I'm getting hungry. Why don't we head over to OST?"

They agreed, so we got up to leave. As we were leaving, Big Lou turned to Dakota and said, "You really like the Captain, don't you?"

She looked uncharacteristically surprised, and I thought I saw her cheeks turn red as she responded, "Yeah."

I tried to pretend I hadn't heard, but Big Lou would have none of it. "Captain," he said, "if ya plan to ever get yer head out of yer ass, she would be a good place to start."

"Good idea," I responded without thinking and walked over and put my arm around Dakota. She leaned into me, smiled and said, "Did I ever tell you I think men who ride with collared shirts are sexy?"

I had already noticed Big Lou had one on, but I didn't care. I was just happy I wore mine. Big Lou came over and put his arm around me, and the three of us marched as one to our motorcycles. Life was good.

OST

OST stands for Old Spanish Trail. It is a restaurant with a great history. But more important to riders, it is *the* place in Bandera. The town bills itself as the Cowboy Capital of the World. There really are a lot of cowboys in the area, but unlike Junction, most of them don't actually work on a ranch anymore. Bandera is a big destination for tourists and motorcycle riders alike, and the OST is everyone's favorite place to eat. It is famous for its buffet meals and chicken fried steak, but it's also one of the friendliest places in the Hill Country. It's usually pretty busy, too.

Surprisingly, Big Lou had never been there. He said he usually didn't ride in this direction and when he did he just continued on to San Antonio, which was only forty miles away.

When we pulled up across the street from the OST and parked, I remembered I had forgotten to check messages on my cell phone, so I told Dakota and Big Lou to go in and I'd catch up with them. Dakota said she needed to check her phone, too. Big Lou said something about leaving us two lovers alone and went across the street to the restaurant.

I had three calls, but nothing important. So I put my phone back in my pack and waited for Dakota to finish a conversation with her shop. While we were standing there two police cars pulled up quietly and parked in front of the entrance, blocking traffic on the usually busy street. Four officers got out and positioned themselves behind their cars. Another police car pulled in and parked between us and the restaurant. Something was wrong.

The next thing I knew, Big Lou came out the front door with a shotgun. Everyone was yelling. Then there was a loud boom-boom and Big Lou fell back against the door and slid to the sidewalk, bleeding badly.

Witnesses inside said the place was full of families. When Big Lou walked in there was an armed robbery taking place. Some of the children were whimpering, and everyone else was pretty much frozen with fear. They said he looked bored by what was happening and just kept walking toward the closest thief. The guy pointed his sawed off shotgun at him and was screaming for him to stop, but Big Lou just walked up and smashed him in the face and took his weapon. He smashed the guy in the head again with the butt and quickly turned toward the other thief, who was running for his life out the back. Big Lou yelled, "Secure this asshole" to some guys sitting on the saddles at the bar, then turned and ran out the front door. They figured he was going to head off the other robber. I have always thought he was coming out to make sure the two of us were safe.

Big Lou didn't realize the manager had tripped a silent alarm or that the police had already arrived. The responding officers had no idea he had disarmed one of the thieves. They just saw a crusty, determined man wielding a lethal weapon. I heard the officers yell, "Halt, drop your weapon!" I saw the surprised look on Big Lou's face as he instinctively raised the shotgun. I heard two gunshots and Dakota's scream, and then I heard my own voice yell, "No!" I have relived those moments in my mind a thousand times. What we had witnessed was a tragic accident. Like most such experiences, those who survived would never be the same.

We rode over to the hospital in one of the police cars, hoping the paramedics would perform a miracle en route. When we arrived a doctor confirmed what we already knew. Big Lou was dead. Detectives took Dakota and me to separate rooms in the hospital and had us write out witness statements. When we finished I was surprised to see Sheriff Gonzalez waiting for us in the visitor's area. We were in another county and well outside his jurisdiction, but it quickly became clear he was not there for business reasons. He was upset, too, and wanted to talk.

In our conversations, Big Lou had verified that most of the stories I had heard about him and the sheriff were true. I had always considered it odd that two such different people could form such a strong friendship. However, in the last few days my superficial view of life had been shattered, and beneath it I found a whole new world. Theirs was not a simple friendship between a biker and a sheriff, but a bond between two people who shared similar values. I was beginning to understand that despite outward appearances, they were very much alike. I found myself wishing I were the same way.

"Big Lou was my friend," the sheriff said, as though he were struggling to find the right words.

"I know," I said. "He told me about your friendship."

"Damn city," he said. I assumed he was referring to the city police, who had done the shooting.

"It was a terrible accident, sir," I said.

"Accidents happen when you give untrained people authority," he said.

"Did they get the bastards?" Dakota asked.

"They got the two kids that did the robbery," the sheriff said. "They are younger than you. We'll put 'em away for a long time, but that ain't gonna help the officer who made the mistake or his family, or you or me or Big Lou. He was a true citizen warrior, and it was our own system that killed him." He sat looking at the tiled floor with his hat in his hand, talking more to himself than to us.

I looked at Dakota. She had tears in her eyes and didn't respond. I couldn't think of a thing to say either.

Finally, the sheriff looked up at me and said, "How were you two doing on our little project?"

"What project?" I asked.

"Remember a couple of months ago one of my motorcycle officers was injured escorting a bunch of riders participating in a charity event?" he said.

"I remember," Dakota said. "I was there. There were about fifty of us. We took off and didn't even make it five blocks. The officer was coming from the intersection we just went through and was passing the group trying to rush to the next crossroad so he could block it before we arrived. A rider toward the front decided he wanted to help so he pulled out of the group, right into the path of your officer. Wham! They both ended up in the hospital."

"I wasn't there," I said, "but I heard about it."

"So did I," the sheriff said. "We totaled a county motorcycle, lost the officer for a month with a broken collar bone and the guy he hit sued the county. The commissioners passed a resolution forbidding me to ever provide an escort again."

"What does that have to do with me?" I asked.

"Hangman was really pissed at the riders and the commissioners. He told the commissioners they should clamp the nuts on the lead sheep, which he figured was whoever was in charge of the run, not cut the nuts off the entire county. Needless to say, they didn't take kindly to his recommendations. But they didn't have the balls to deny him completely, so they told him to bring back a plan and they would reconsider.

"Immediately after the meeting he had me go pick up Big Lou and meet him at his house. I don't ride anymore, but all three of us were riders back in the old days and knew what the problem was. We just needed to figure out how to fix it."

"What was the problem?" Dakota asked.

"Leadership," the sheriff said. Then he continued, "That night after the commissioners meeting, we decided to pick one rider with leadership potential and let Big Lou give them a little dose of reality. He insisted you be that rider."

"Why me?" I asked.

"I don't know," he said. "He always seemed interested in what you were doing. I guess he must a seen something in you, and he sure must trust you. I've never known him to ride with anyone around here."

"He was teaching me a few things," I said. I was feeling completely exhausted and close to loosing it. Choking back tears I said, "Look, I can't talk anymore right now. Maybe tomorrow."

The sheriff offered to take us to a motel and promised to see that someone would take care of our bikes. Dakota agreed. When he dropped us off at the motel, he said he would pick us up for breakfast in the morning. It was clear this was a personal loss for him, too.

So when he said he would be there for us at zero eight hundred hours in the morning, I remembered how I had used the same words with such false bravado to invite Dakota on this ride and how Big Lou had used the same phrase so naturally just two days before. I wondered why he had decided I was worth teaching and why he was dead. Then I lost it.

Dakota helped me into the room, and we spent our first night together crying, talking and sleeping. The next day we had breakfast with the sheriff, and he assured us he had taken care of Big Lou's motorcycle. He also said he would try to find Big Lou's family. Dakota and I took Highway 16 to Kerrville, hopped on I-10 and got home as fast as we could. We stopped at her place and sent an email and made calls to our riding group to let them know about Big Lou and that the ride for Sunday was canceled. Before I left for home I kissed her and said, "I think I love you." She looked me in the eyes and said, "Call me when you know for sure."

I went to my motorcycle, retrieved my cell phone and called her.

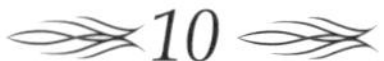

10

Leading Big Lou's Way

Lou was buried at Fort Sam Houston National Cemetery in San Antonio with full military honors. Since he was buried on Tuesday, not many people were in attendance. About a dozen of our riders and about twenty from other groups were there along with several deputies from the Sheriff's Department and an American Legion Honor Guard. The sheriff wasn't able to locate any family, so he and his wife, Hangman and Dakota and I filled in. My mother came, too. I felt an overwhelming sadness. The sound of the rifle salute, listening to Taps and watching the flag folded and handed to the sheriff didn't help. *The wisdom of this complicated, ornery, principled man cannot die with him,* I thought. I pledged to myself that from that day forward, it would be my mission to see that his legend and all that he taught me lived on.

Dakota and I had spent the three days before his funeral holed up at my place. We talked a lot about life, Big Lou and us. We had also discussed planning a memorial ride for him. After the service we both knew what we had to do.

That night and the next morning Dakota and I developed a plan. We would take our group on a ride to Bandera the next Sunday. At OST we would tell them of our plan for an annual memorial ride and solicit their help.

"This is not going to be a half-assed motorcycle traffic jam," I said. "This is going to be like the ride we took with Big Lou. Everyone is going to know what's going on and agree to some rules before we leave. I want him to look down and wish he was riding with us."

"Yes sir, Captain," she said, and then added, "I love you."

I looked up and said, "Thank you, Big Lou."

Later that day I went to see Hangman. When I mentioned to him at the funeral that I planned to do some kind of ride to honor Big Lou, he had said, "I don't wanna know." It had been bothering me since, so I decided to stop by and ask what he meant. He wasn't in his "office" on the front porch so I knocked on the front door. After a few seconds the door opened. Hangman was standing there in his boxer shorts and no shirt with shotgun in hand. It was about as ugly a sight as I had ever seen.

"Office is closed," he growled.

"I'm not here on business," I said. "I'm here to invite you to a run to Bandera on Sunday."

"I told you I don't wanna know that shit," he said. "Now get the hell outta here." He shut the door.

I had no idea what his problem was, but I really didn't care. I had made the courtesy visit Big Lou had told me to make. *Job done, hell with that fat old bastard,* I thought, then immediately looked up at the sky and said, "Sorry, Big Lou. I'll keep working on my attitude."

A Shocking Discovery

Later that same afternoon Sheriff Gonzalez called and asked me to meet him at Big Lou's house. Dakota tagged along, and when we got there he handed me a letter. It was postmarked 1971 and addressed to Sgt.

Louis "Chief" Stone, E Troop 1st Cavalry, APO San Francisco 96374. The return address said simply, Sgt. M. Whitehorse. The letter inside was brief:

> *Chief,*
> *I am in the San Antonio Airport and on my way. I decided to race this letter to you. Watch your back until I get there. See you soon.*
> *Point*
> *P.S. Met the love of my life at the Dairy Queen in Kerrville on the way to the Airport.*

I knew that Whitehorse called Big Lou "Chief" and that he called Whitehorse "Point." He had told me the story and explained that Point was a term for the first person on a patrol in Vietnam. It was considered dangerous, but Whitehorse had always volunteered for the job.

My heart jumped, and I rechecked the postmark. January 28, 1971. Nine months before I was born. I handed the letter to Dakota, but I couldn't talk. As she read it, tears were streaming down her cheeks. I had told her my mother's story, and in the past few days they had talked on the phone, one time for over an hour. The sheriff was sitting in Big Lou's chair, and Dakota and I were on the couch. My mind was racing so fast I didn't notice the silence or the fact that they were waiting for me to speak.

It isn't possible, I thought. My mother had always told me my father's name was Mike Kountz, but she never said anything to indicate he might have had Indian blood or been in the military. The more I thought about it the more unlikely it became.

"Where did you get this?" I finally asked the sheriff.

"In a box in the bedroom, along with his medals and a .38 caliber pistol and a New Testament," he said. "Not much else in the bedroom but some clothes. He wasn't much for keepin' things he couldn't carry on his motorcycle."

"This is bullshit," I said, suddenly feeling as if my back were against some kind of wall. "Did you know about this before today?" I asked the sheriff.

"Not exactly," he said. "Before he moved here, he called me several times and asked a bunch of questions about your mother and you, so I knew he was interested in you for some reason."

"You knew Big Lou before he moved here?" Dakota asked.

"Yes," he said. "It's a long story, but he and the judge and I go back a long way."

"If he thought there was a chance Josh was Michael Whitehorse's son, why wouldn't he say something?" Dakota asked.

"He wasn't the kind of guy who got involved in other people's business," I said. "I know that much. And I know that he and Whitehorse never saw each other again. Big Lou had been wounded and was in the hospital in Saigon when he arrived. Whitehorse was sent on a special assignment to the border with Laos and was killed before they could get back together."

"I know he talked to your mother, Josh. But I don't know what they talked about," the sheriff said.

"She never said anything to me," I said. My emotions were bouncing from heartsick to anger to numbing shock and back again. I loved my mother and I realized she knew Big Lou, but I couldn't understand why she wouldn't tell me if she had talked to him about something so personal.

"One more thing, Josh," the sheriff said. "Since Big Lou didn't have family the judge told me to let you have whatever you want, then sell the rest before Austin finds out."

"I don't want..." I said, stopping myself in mid sentence. "All I want is the framed feather and note on the kitchen wall."

We walked to the kitchen, and he took the frame off the wall and handed it to me.

"Keep it safe," he said with complete seriousness.

I handed it to Dakota in hopes of keeping my emotions in check. But it didn't work. As she read the note, tears were streaming down her face, and soon mine started flowing, too.

When we got home, I immediately called my mother. She sounded very uncomfortable when I started questioning her about Michael Whitehorse and her relationship with Big Lou.

"Yes," she said, "I have seen the letter. Big Lou showed it to me just before he moved to Junction."

"You knew Big Lou before he moved here?" I said.

"He came to town when you were about nine years old and showed me the letter. He said it was none of his business, but he knew I had worked at the Dairy Queen in Kerrville and wondered if I could recall ever meeting a friend of his named Michael Whitehorse. I told him no. Then he said his friend was a real jokester and could have given me another name."

"Big Lou told me about that," I said. "He said Whitehorse got a kick out of being half-Indian and half-white. He would tell Big Lou he was going undercover as a white man and change his last name for the night."

"I told him your father was not a liar," she said. "He

told me he was sorry to intrude and that he just happened to be in the area looking at historic markers and noticed one with the name Kountz on it. Then he said he wouldn't bother me anymore and that was it. He left. Later I was surprised when he moved to Junction. We said hello once in a while, and I took you to see him before you got your first motorcycle, but he never brought the subject up with me again."

"Mom, was Michael Whitehorse my father?" I asked.

"Josh, you are my whole life," she said, sounding on the verge of tears. "Your father was not a liar," she added and hung up.

It bothered me that I had upset her, but I was upset, too. I shared our conversation with Dakota, and she remembered the historic marker for Isaac Kountz out on 377 just outside of town. We decided to ride out and take a look. In polished letters on the bronze legend plate was the following information:

> *Isaac Kountz - Killed on this spot by Indians on Christmas Eve, 1867. He was 16 years old, and herding sheep for his father, Dr. E.K. Kountz. A brother, Sebastian, Age 11, escaped. A posse and Texas Rangers chased the Indians to the Guadalupe River. Young Kountz was buried in Junction Cemetery.*

Dakota and I stood there holding each other, and we talked. Did Michael Whitehorse pass by this same marker? It was a very popular road for motorcycle riders. From the little I knew about him he would have gotten a kick out of using the name Kountz. Was it a coincidence that my father's name was Mike Kountz?

After we fell silent for a while, Dakota said, "Josh,

what are you feeling right now?"

I thought about her question for a moment and pushed my ego aside, taking a good look within. I did not like what I saw. I had not been thinking about Dakota or my mother or Big Lou or anyone other than myself. I had forgotten the people I care about and was focused entirely on me. It was one of the habits Big Lou had helped me see in myself and one I found very disappointing. I had pledged to the mirror that I would change. But there I was sinking back to my old ways.

"I feel selfish and embarrassed," I said.

"Why?" she asked.

"Big Lou would never have made that call to my mother today," I said. "I shouldn't have, and if I wasn't only thinking about myself I wouldn't have either. He would have said, 'It don't mean nothin,' and he would have been right. My mother deserves to have her memories however she chooses. It doesn't matter if Whitehorse was my father or not. It doesn't change who I am. I can't waste my time worrying about the past or feeling sorry for myself. I need to move forward. What matters is that the things Big Lou taught me don't get lost. I have the feather now, and I need to get my head out of my ass."

"What?" she said, "You mean your shoulders won't be in the way when I look at your beautiful ass?" Then she pinched me on the butt and I pinched her back. The next thing we knew we were running around chasing each other, childishly pinching one another and giggling.

When we got home I called my mother. She was at work so I left a message telling her I loved her. Dakota and I went to bed early, and our childish pinching resumed until passion turned our giggling into heavy breathing and our touches became soft and warm. Later that night I awoke and was watching her as she slept when I thought, *If I can get my head out of my ass, this unbelievable women sleeping next to me could be the mother of my children. Thank you, God… and you, too, Big Lou.*

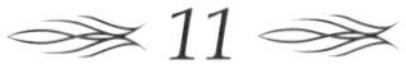

11

Big Lou's Ride

Both Dakota and I went back to work on Thursday. My boss had a change of heart for some reason and gave me my old job back along with a token raise, but I really didn't care. I had only two things on my mind: Dakota and Sunday's ride.

We had sent out an email and made calls setting the assembly time at Issack's Restaurant for zero eight thirty hours with a briefing at zero nine hundred hours and departure at zero nine fifteen. I had asked Stinky to be the assistant lead bike and Mad Dog to "sweep" and told them both to show up a little early. A "sweep" is the last motorcycle, and it's that rider's job to help manage the discipline of the group and assist anyone who may have a breakdown or emergency. Sometimes riders also call the job "tail gunner."

I have already told you about Stinky, and there isn't much to tell about Mad Dog. He was about forty-five years old with a full red beard. His hair fell just over his ears and was sort of tangled in with his beard and a generous crop of black ear hair. He was about five foot seven inches tall with a very broad muscular build. If you were meeting him for the first time, you would think "Mad Dog" was a perfect description of his appearance and personality. He was also fiercely loyal to his friends, so if ever there was trouble brewing you could bet he would be in the middle of it. Although he would never intentionally start a conflict, he left no doubt about his willingness to end one. Like often happens in riding groups, despite the fact I knew him pretty well, I had no idea what his real name was.

Dakota and I had discussed the fact that I would be the ride leader, but I wanted her to be the first bike. She was at least as skilled as I was as a rider, and I wanted to watch the group before we started picking a team for the memorial ride. Fingers had agreed to use his tow-truck as a chase vehicle, which made Comfort happy. A chase vehicle travels behind the group and provides assistance in the event of a breakdown. Sometimes they pick up the broken bike and take it for repairs, other times they will secure the area behind the motorcycle until it is fixed or can be pushed to a safe place. Although we occasionally had people follow us on runs, we had never designated anyone as a chase vehicle before. In fact, I didn't know there was such a thing until I started looking for answers to Big Lou's questions on the Internet.

Stinky, Mad Dog and Fingers were already there when Dakota and I arrived. I went over the plan and asked if they had any questions. Mad Dog was a very experienced rider who, as I mentioned before, used to belong to an MC. It was a fact he shared with the rest of us whenever possible.

"What the hell's got into your ass?" he asked. "First time anybody in this group ever bothered to do shit right. When I was ridin' with the club, they taught you the rules before they let you ride. Ridin' with these idiots could get you killed, that's why I always ride in the back."

"I know, Mad Dog. You've said that before. That's why I need you and Fingers on the team. Most of our group hasn't been trained like you have. They don't know there's a better way. But I intend to show them, and I need your help."

"You got it, brother," he said. Fingers nodded in agreement.

"Great. I will do the briefing, and I need the four of you to keep an eye on the group. If we have any new people, I want to know about it. If someone's not paying attention, let them know about it. If someone arrives after the briefing, I want them to see me. While kick stands are up, Dakota is in charge. If someone fails to pass along her signals, I want to know about it. If anyone makes any move for any reason other than safety, I want to know about it. We are going to have a fun, safe ride and look good doing it. Got it?" I said.

"Yes sir, Captain," Dakota said.

"Yes sir, Captain," Stinky repeated.

"That's what I'm talkin' about," Mad Dog added.

"God bless you," Fingers added.

When it was time to assemble the group, I got up on the big cement planter by the parking lot. There were twenty-six riders in all. Dakota, Stinky, Mad Dog and Fingers whistled and herded the reluctant group together. Most were mumbling and wondering what was going on. When I started the briefing, several people were grab assin' or talking so Mad Dog whistled and yelled.

"Hey, assholes, yer Road Captain's talking. Let's show some respect."

Things quieted down, and I continued with the briefing. When I got to the part about "no racing" there was a little applause. When I mentioned that anyone who didn't want to follow the ride rules should leave the group and meet us in Bandera, there were a few grumbles. Generally, however, they were just surprised. They had never had a pre-ride briefing before, and they didn't recognize the person giving it. Then again, they didn't really know Big Lou.

Because of the number of riders, I asked Toad to serve as a unit leader and broke the group up into two units. We would ride together as one group, but if we encountered traffic Toad would be in position to create a gap and lead the back half of the motorcycles. Traffic wasn't a real problem in our county on Sunday morning, except immediately after the church services, but I wanted to be prepared just in case.

We had decided to stop in Leakey so Dakota pulled into the designated gas station, just past the turn for Road 337. She had been doing a great job keeping a smooth, steady pace. A couple of riders had not been passing along signals so I sent Mad Dog to have a word with them. That was a mistake. Mad Dog's interpersonal communication skills left a lot to be desired, and he was soon barking orders like a… mad dog. To make matters worse, he was talking to a husband and wife. When I walked up, the wife was crying and the husband was about to punch Mad Dog. Instead he turned to me and got right in my face.

"I'm going to kick his ass and yours, too," he said.

He was a fair-sized guy, with a large beer belly. I figured if something started, he would be out of breath in short order. I instantly thought of Big Lou and realized he had prepared me for this situation. Without lowering my gaze I spoke calmly. "Bullshit," I said. "Look, this isn't about you or me or Mad Dog, it's about the safety of the group. You need to pass the signals along. Do you understand why we need you to do it?"

"Yeah, sure, but that doesn't give this asshole the right to talk to us like he did."

"Sorry, man," Mad Dog chimed in. "I didn't mean

no disrespect. I'm just tryin' to do my job."

"Well, you suck at it," the guy responded.

"So, what's it going to be?" I asked. "You in or out? You can meet us in Bandera or stay with us. You are welcome either way. It's not personal. Anyone who doesn't contribute to the group gets a visit from Mad Dog. He's doing his job the best he knows how. All we ask is that you do the best you can, too."

"This is a bunch of crap," he said. "I've been ridin' since before you were born. Nobody tells me what to do."

I knew from my experience with Big Lou that his ego had been bruised and he was not going to give in, especially with his wife looking on.

"Then we'll see you in Bandera," I said.

"Hey, gang," he yelled. "Anyone who's tired of this bullshit, we're formin' our own ride. Come with us."

Nobody moved so he rode off with his wife, who was now protesting his decision. Dakota and Stinky looked over at me and smiled, and Mad Dog slapped me on the back and said, "Let's ride, brother."

The rest of the ride to Bandera was a thing of beauty. The group was communicating and riding together better than I had ever seen. They were keeping the appropriate intervals, and nobody was falling behind. No one was racing or running up on the rider ahead or making any moves independent of the others. Despite the fact that the area is mostly free range and full of domestic, wild and exotic animals as well as falling rocks, they didn't hit anything or target fixate and run off the road. Nobody even panicked around the ever-present turkey buzzards that keep the roads clean along that route.

It was a beautiful ride. I hoped Big Lou could see

what he had done. As we turned onto Highway 16 in Medina three motorcycle cops raced by and pulled in front of Dakota. They formed a wedge and turned on their lights and sirens. In my mirror I saw Sheriff Gonzalez pull in behind me and in front of Fingers, who had dropped back quite a distance with his tow-truck. The sheriff was giving me the thumbs up. Despite the fact that we were three counties from home, our little group from Junction would arrive in Bandera in style.

When we reached OST there were at least five hundred people waiting. I felt proud and confused and overwhelmed, and tears began to well up in my eyes. The city of Bandera had an area coned off in the street with a sign that read BIG LOU'S MOTORCYCLES ONLY. It was all the more remarkable because it was the main street and normally had lots of tourist traffic.

Once we were parked, I headed straight toward the front of the group looking for Dakota. She still had her helmet on and was running toward me. We hugged and I said, "Take your damn helmet off so I can kiss you."

She said, "I don't want these assholes to see me crying."

"Who gives a shit?" I said, the tears streaming down my cheeks.

She said, "I love you," as she took off her helmet and gave me a kiss. Mad Dog, Toad and Stinky came up, and we shared hugs all around. Mad Dog gave me a fake punch in the gut and said, "I didn't know you two were screwin'."

Dakota smiled and said, "Mad Dog, you've been married six times and still don't know what love looks like?"

Mad Dog's big hairy cheeks turned bright red, and

he mumbled, "Only been married five times. I'd rather be gay than make that mistake again." He promptly turned to Stinky, grabbed his ears and gave him a big kiss on the lips. Stinky immediately started spitting, and our pent up emotions exploded in the form of laughter.

Fingers, Comfort and the sheriff came over and joined us. Fingers had become quite fond of the sheriff since his experience in jail. As soon as they arrived he said, "I need to take up a collection for the government guys and put out his skull cap. They need eighteen bucks."

"Fingers, haven't you gotten your safety inspection sticker on that truck yet? I told you about that six months ago," the sheriff said.

"Yes sir, you sure did," Fingers said. "I plum forgot 'til I saw ya in my mirror back there a piece. When I sees ya'll I said to Comfort, Lord forgive me, I done forgot that sticker and pissed off my friend the sheriff. Sure was happy to see you go by."

The sheriff just shook his head, and while he was doing it, Hangman came up.

"Sheriff," he said, "what the hell all these motorcycles and half the voters in our county doin' here?"

"Got me," the sheriff said. "All I know is I got a call from Bandera County askin' for help with some traffic. Was there a motorcycle run today?"

"Not that I know of," Hangman said. "Good fortune you and your deputies were available to help. It gave ya a chance to test yer new escort plan to boot. Looks like everything works great. I am lookin' forward to tellin' the commissioners another county adopted the plan before they did. "

We hung around the parking lot for almost an hour,

first hugging one another, then mixing and talking with the crowd. I found out later that Dakota had called both the restaurant manager and Sheriff Gonzalez to let them know we were riding to Bandera to plan a memorial ride for Big Lou. They had taken it from there. All the people who had been at OST the day Big Lou saved them from the robbery were there, along with their families, relatives and friends. With that one heroic act, he had impacted a lot of lives. I couldn't help but wonder how many others he had touched in his life.

When we entered the restaurant we found the manager had coned off the whole back room for us and marked it with a sign that read, "Big Lou's Crew." I sat in the corner with my back to the wall and told the group a couple of stories about Big Lou and what he had taught me. It didn't go like stories about him usually went. No one tried to outdo me. No one interrupted. When I finished, I thanked Dakota, Stinky, Mad Dog, Fingers and Toad and then the entire group for the great ride. One of the riders stood up and said, "Why don't we do some kind of memorial run to honor Big Lou?"

I said, "Dakota, would you please explain our plan." With those words, my mission in life began, and it has been an incredible ride. But that's another story.

Epilogue

I'm working on the story of Big Lou's life, as he told it to me, so I can't tell you a lot about my own adventures right now. But here's an update.

We created a memorial event in Big Lou's honor the year following his death. It's called the Eagle Feather Run and is now held every April in the Texas Hill Country. Hundreds of riders participate each year, and it raises a lot of money for Wounded Warriors and their families. It has gotten too big for our little riding group to handle alone, so they still do the organizing while a group of American Legion Riders out of San Antonio helps make it happen. They spend a lot of time serving others, but otherwise are a lot like us—just a bunch of good people who like to ride, not a club or association or anything.

Our group still doesn't have a name, but it continues to grow and has remained active, its members participating in a lot of charity rides together. Since the ride to Bandera to plan Big Lou's memorial run, they have never had a problem with racing or disorganization again. They no longer follow someone just because everyone else does. They ask questions and require their Road Captains to complete a training program. They make sure new riders know what to expect and what is expected of them before kick stands go up. Those riders who choose not to give up their individualism to fit in aren't allowed to ride with the group, although they are welcomed at destinations.

The sheriff says our county has the best group riders in the state of Texas. Other riders say our group is as easy and fun to ride with as any traditional riding club or association. In case you are like I was and haven't found a real group to ride with yet, I have included my notes on some of the stuff Big Lou taught me and my first pre-ride briefing. I have used them many times since. Mad Dog used them to form a little company that organizes group rides across the country. I think Big Lou would be happy.

Fingers and Comfort figured out some riders will stop anyplace they see other bikes, so they started a Bikers Church. Services are held in Telegraph at the Telegraph Store and Post Office. It's not hard to find if you happen to be up that way. It's located a short ride west of Junction on 377, and it's the only building in Telegraph. If it's not open, just sit out front on the old car seat until somebody shows up. The Sheriff's Department chaplin officiates so you might want to pick up a lunch to-go from Isaack's Restaurant before you head that way.

The sheriff retired the year of Big Lou's death but still works his exotic wildlife ranch west of town. He has quite an assortment of animals but hasn't opened up the place to hunting like everyone else. He says he would rather look at nature than the ass end of a bunch of hunters. We stay in touch.

Hangman's still "fighting crime and government pissants" and wants to make sure I tell riders ya'll are welcome in Kimble County. He says his revenue is down a little this year so he could use the customers. He's getting up there in years, but it hasn't watered down his potent ways.

Stinky is doing great. His company has grown so

much they bought Mr. Dunn's company and fired him. Toad now runs that business and still owns the computer business, too. Jimmy and Ace are doing well and have three kids now. Jimmy is a full professor.

I rarely get to ride with the group anymore. If I'm not out of the country I always make the Eagle Feather Run, but otherwise I'm pretty busy. About two months after Big Lou died, I joined the Air Force and Dakota enrolled in nursing school. We were married shortly after I completed Officers Candidate School. We had a few rough years spending a lot of time apart as we pursued our education and careers, but things are good now and we appreciate each other more than ever.

Life is good, but I'll always be a little embarrassed about how serious I was back then, about myself and the little things that, as my mentor would say, "Don't mean nothin'." I'm still a bit of a technology nerd, but I no longer look at life as a series of plug-and-play programs created for my convenience. I also understand that there are realities in life that don't change just because I'm on my motorcycle or computer. Big Lou taught me how to keep my head up, where to look and how to recognize danger ahead. He helped me accept the fact that I am responsible for twisting my own throttle, on my motorcycle and in life. In the process he helped me see citizenship, leadership and other people in a whole new light. It's amazing to me how often I use his lessons, both while riding and while living.

To this day, whenever I go into a meeting, I imagine everyone in the room is on a motorcycle and we are about to leave for a ride. Try it sometime. You may be surprised at how easy it is to determine if you are about to embark on an adventurous journey or a dangerous trip with a pack of lone wolves. As Big Lou said,

"Ya can learn more about life in one day ridin' a motorcycle than a lifetime a listenin' ta fancy talkers or starin' at a computer." I sure do miss him.

Ride Safe, Ride Old,
—Josh "Captain" Dery, Major, U.S. Air Force

SNAPSHOTS

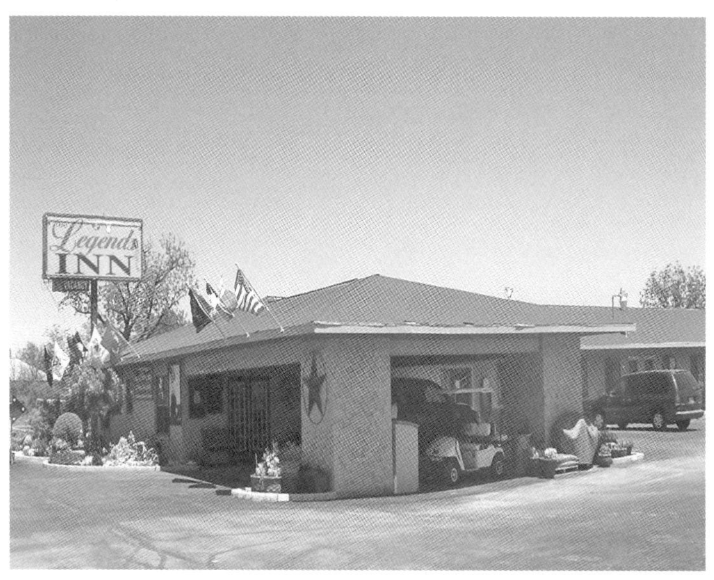

The Legends Inn. A popular place to stay when riding the Texas Hill Country.

Issack's Restaurant.
A regular hangout for local riders.

The Willow Creek Cafe in Mason County.
A regular lunch stop for riders.

London Hall, London, TX, just east of Junction.
The other "big city" in Kimble County.

The Junction Restaurant is right off I-10 at Exit 456. Good people and good food.

Kimble County Line. Riders are welcome but had better behave. A visit to the justice of the peace can be a very expensive experience.

The Isaac Kountz historical marker is located just west of the Junction city limits on Highway 377.

Exotic animals are a common site on the run between Junction and Bandera. There is also domestic stock, wildlife and lots of free range. Ride with your head and eyes up and during daylight hours only.

The three Twisted Sisters are scenic roads with many twists, turns, switchbacks and steep grades. To enjoy a great trip, look where you want to go and watch your entry speed in corners. Take your time and pull over regularly to take in the beauty.

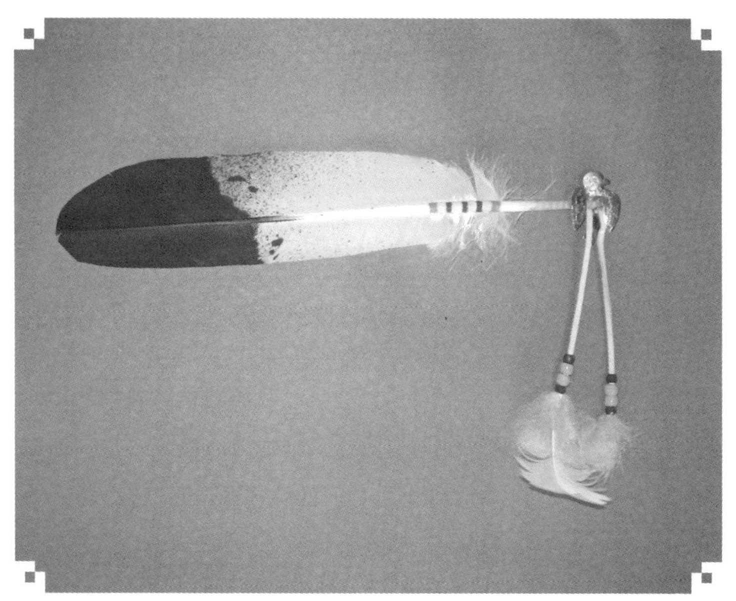

NOTES

1. **Riding is riding and groups are groups.** *Riding skills determine the formation, pace and route. Group management skills determine rules, attitudes and benefits.*

2. **You can't blame motorcycles for who you are**. *We are all responsible for our individual actions. Machines and technology make us faster, not better.*

3. **Anybody can go fast.** *Speed is not a skill. Knowing when and where to use it is.*

4. **Know your route.** *Never follow a leader unless you understand where they are going and why.*

5. **Know your destination.** *Determine where you want to go and why. Then stay on the right road.*

6. **Observe those around you.** *Understand how and why they are there and prepare for what they will do next.*

7. **Don't let anyone else twist your throttle.** *If you worry about what others think you will never be free or safe.*

8. **Check your mirrors, but never look back.** *Spending too much time worrying about what's behind you takes your eyes off the road ahead.*

9. **Respect the danger ahead.** *You are your own worst enemy when you take your eyes off the road.*

10. ***Never ride with your head up your ass!***

Big Lou on Group Leadership

This is my translation of Big Lou's ten points about leading. They are truths that he said were well understood by leaders of most motorcycle groups, even the worst of the outlaws, but had been lost on me and many new riders.

1. The nature of groups requires some level of conformity by all participants.

2. All groups require rules to define conformity.

3. Resistance to rules is natural.

4. All participants will weigh the benefits of participation against the cost of conformity.

5. Some will try to reap the benefits of participation without paying the cost of conformity.

6. Uncompromising individualism is a threat to the group.

7. Disciplined, mission-focused leadership is essential to group success.

8. Communication is a primal tool in all group success.

9. Group structure, planning and team building are key elements to leadership success.

10. Good group leadership is never personal. Group participation is always personal.

Big Lou's 15-Point Pre-ride Briefing

1. Ride team introduction:

Introduce your team, including the Lead Road Captain, Assistant Road Captain, Unit Road Captains, Tail Gunner, Chase Team and others on the ride team. The primary purpose is to make sure the group knows you are not just a "lone wolf" trying to take over the pack.

2. Today's destination is:

Explain the objectives for the ride, where and why you are going and what will happen when you get there.

3. The route is:

Let everyone know that there is a ride plan. Give as much detail as possible about each planned stop. The more each individual rider knows, the more likely they will not leave the group while rolling.

4. Unique road conditions:

Note constructions, traffic and other factors that may involve individual rider decisions. The more they know ahead of time, the easier it will be to stay together.

5. Weather forecast:

Recommend solutions like sunscreen, eye drops, hydration, rain gear or other factors unique to the ride. Do not assume the needs are obvious. Someone in the group will use your reminder to make personal decisions.

6. Ride with a buddy:

This is a group ride. Have each rider pick a buddy. They should stay together for the entire ride. It's the best way to manage against a "lone wolf" getting into the middle of the pack.

7. Pull over procedures:
Advise the group that only the rider and riding buddy are to pull over in an emergency. The remainder of the group should proceed to a safe place, such as an exit or parking lot. Remind those pulling over to turn on their emergency flashers and advise them of the procedure for signaling the chase vehicle.

8. Riding formation:
Explain the formation the ride will use. If staggered, discuss intervals and if there will be automatic changes for rain or other road conditions. Remind riders to reduce the slingshot effect by using steady throttle movements and staying off brakes as much as possible. Also encourage them to catch up slowly (Don't throttle away from the rider behind.) This is also a good place to discuss other matters related to the formation, such as special locations for trikes and trailers, or new riders.

9. Use hand signals:
Review all hand signals that will be used on the ride, even if the group rides together often. It ensures all riders are current and guarantees new riders are informed. Place emphasis on the importance of acknowledging and passing along all signals.

10. Check your pack:
Reminded them of the importance of checking packs and saddlebags. It is critical to the safety of the group.

11. Group rules:
Review any special rules and cover policies such as, alcohol, attitudes, racing, side by side riding and other matters. You should also explain the reason for each rule.

12. **Riders are responsible for their own safety:** *Make sure the riders know they should not exceed their riding skills. Remind them not to allow anyone else to twist their throttle and that their decisions will impact the rest of the group.*

13. **Keep up and follow the rules or go it alone:** *Inform riders that if they are having trouble keeping up or do not wish to conform to the ride rule, they should leave the group and proceed at their own pace. They can meet you at the next stop.*

14. **Confirm who's in charge:** *Let them know the Road Captain and/or ride leader's decisions will be final in all matters concerning your group ride. If they are not completely comfortable they should leave the group before departure and meet at the next stop. It's okay!*

15. **Confirm group agreement:** *Ask for questions. Ask if everyone understands and agrees to the ride rules. Make sure everyone understands the liability standard for the ride. Have the group confirm their agreement verbally.*

This series was created to promote public awareness and conversation about motorcycle safety using an entertainment venue. The stories are works of fiction, yet the importance of motorcycle safety is very real.

It is the responsibility of all of us, riders and non-riders alike, to understand the nature of motorcycling free of myths. In reality, no matter how fast we go or which transportation we choose, we cannot escape the fact that we are human. We should not set expectations of one another otherwise.

Non-riders have every right to expect motorcyclists to respect and conform to the rules of the road. At the same time, they need to understand how and why riding a motorcycle differs from driving.

Riders have every right to expect other vehicles to share our highways with awareness and safe driving habits. But we must respect the reality that Mother Nature doesn't change the rules because we are on a motorcycle.

We can all be safer on our roads if we take time to understand one another and separate fact from fiction. There are associations and clubs for motorcyclists as well as for drivers, with expertise in safety. Learn the facts from these experts. Join the discussion. Be part of the solution. Get involved and have some serious fun!

—T. J. Haynes